Hurry Home

John Edgar Wideman

Hurry Home

An Owl Book

HENRY HOLT AND COMPANY • NEW YORK

PS
3573
.I26
H8
1986

Published by Henry Holt and Company,
521 Fifth Avenue, New York, New York 10175.
Published simultaneously in Canada.

Library of Congress Cataloging-in-Publication Data
Wideman, John Edgar.
Hurry home.
I. Title.
PS3573.I26H8   1986   813'.54   85-27206
ISBN 0-03-005242-4 (pbk.)

First published in hardcover by Harcourt Brace
Jovanovich, Inc., in 1970.

First Owl Book Edition—1986

Printed in the United States of America
1 3 5 7 9 10 8 6 4 2

ISBN 0-03-005242-4

For Judy

. . . *I should call this being*
In love with you
This skipping backwards
And forwards and quiet litanizing
Of fears

1

CECIL CRUSHED IN HIS HANDS THE EMPTY
Carnation evaporated milk can. It was red and white and
decorated with a tiny picture of a flower. Every morning
the garbage had to go down. Five floors, fifteen apartments
each left their bundles on the back staircase for Cecil to
cart away. Striding flight by flight Cecil used the stairs because the real estate agency didn't want the smell of garbage in the tenants' elevator. Some mornings Cecil dreamed
while he carted, but sometimes he thought black thoughts
and handled the trash bags as if he could hurt them. Often
Cecil was drunk in the mornings, stumbling up and down
the dimly lighted back stairs, spilling cans and greasy paper,
slipping on the mess he'd made beneath his feet. Cecil
talked to himself, cried, cursed, tried to make his voice echo
in the long stairwell. There were times when, two or three
stories up, he would send one of the tenant's bags crashing
to the concrete floor of the basement. The fact that it would
be he and no one else who had to sweep up the broken
glass, mop the slush, and scrape together every morsel of
refuse seemed not to deter him.

For many reasons November 14, 1968, was one of Cecil's most difficult mornings. To begin with his piles were
bad. The sight of his own blood, no matter what the source
or occasion, depressed Cecil with thoughts of death and dis-
solution. The first time he had hit his wife, Esther, was because she had told him there was blood in the toilet bowl he
had forgotten to flush. November 14 also found Cecil suf-

3

fering from a hangover. He swore he would die in November, that it was a month sent specifically to plague him with bad luck and worse. He had lost his first girl friend in November, Esther's aunt had come to live with them in November, his son born dead had been conceived in November, etc., etc., as far back as he could remember. As he grew older Cecil tried to remain as inert as possible during that month. For the past few years after attending to the minimal chores that absolutely had to be attended to at Constance Beauty's or now in his capacity as janitor of the Banbury Street Arms, Cecil took to his bed and bottle when the bad month began. Lying in state, he would stare for hours at the patched and cracking ceiling of his basement apartment. Lumps of unfinished plaster reminded him of relief maps, of faces puckered and blistered by burns.

On November 14 Cecil crushed a can and dropped it five flights to the basement. Long after the clatter had burst up through the dark stairwell and the rattling motion of bent tin rolling across the uneven concrete floor had ceased, Cecil stood peering into the tunnel. In another world Cecil heard a door opening. A shadow flitted across his silence, then the light footfall of a voice. *Why did you do that,* once, twice, and perhaps again. Perhaps his own voice asking, feminine, patient, but turning Cecil saw her in the doorway sleeping though she stood. Sleep resting like the red hair on her shoulders, sleep like a topping of snow spread over a dying city. Cecil thought of how they run movies backward, how the can could leap up from the floor, return to his hand and unfold there, a flower opening. It would be fine and easy, no less real than the red hair, the soft robe open at the throat. Cecil could not speak, could only wait for the next sign. The light behind her carried out into the dim hallway, penetrating what should be her solid form, disintegrating hair, flesh, and robe till what Cecil saw was a shaft of brilliance, dazzling, warning him. Sun through her window, through the sheer wrap. Cecil's stare touched her, told her that his hands could be no more intimate, flagrant on her body. He took one step forward, but still couldn't speak, and the light disappeared.

Cecil descended, pausing at each landing to load his burlap sack. There were mornings when the sack became bloated to capacity, and stooped under its weight Cecil was forced to wrestle his load directly to the basement before all the floors were cleared. The bags of garbage he couldn't manage seemed to jeer at him as he passed, make obscene comments about his bent back and heavy breathing. In November there were always more of these mornings than in any other month. Cecil knew he would have to make two trips as he harvested an overflow of waste on the fifth floor. The women didn't seem to care. They pulled the things out of their bodies and laid them atop the trash cans in full view as casually as they would leave a cigarette tipped with lipstick. Cecil had grown accustomed to filth, to the forlorn crusts of pleasure. Cecil no longer made distinctions, no longer judged; he only became angry when someone's carelessness created practical difficulties for him. Broken glass, an overfilled or wet-bottomed bag that spilled when he tried to lift it.

The cigarette lay cold on his lip. Sack would have to be emptied though two floors and their jesters waited below. The woman on the fifth floor on fire in her doorway. He knew her name, and she knew his and nothing in a year had extended that simple knowledge they had of each other. Most likely she didn't even know his last name because as he tried to recall more than the S. Sherman painted on her mailbox, he realized he didn't know what name the initial S began.

Last two floors could wait awhile he decided, closing the double doors of the garbage bin. He cursed as he heard gospel music eking from his basement flat. Damp batwings flut-

tered against his cheek, brushed his shoulder as he stooped
to avoid his underwear and Esther's hanging outside the
laundry room. Esther up and at it already. *I've got a tele-
phone in my bosom,* was it Sister Rosetta Tharpe who
greeted him as he entered the janitor's quarters. *And I can
ring Him up from my heart.* Then piano, guitar, and chorus
led by a bass exploding deep. Esther. Esther. Cecil dropped
the sack just inside the door, which he had left open behind
him.

    —You want something to eat, Cecil. He knew the ques-
tion was *do you love just this small thing about me, this fact
that I can fill your belly,* but Cecil shook his head no, that
same no that seemed appropriate to all her questions, large
or small. Cecil wondered why it had to be said so many
times. Tried to remember if it had been more difficult to refuse her at the beginning. It must have hurt, must have
taken something out of him that first time, though he
couldn't recall what. Esther hovered beside the stove, patient if he should change his mind, as if he could change it.
Backgrounded by sweet organ music the announcer was
leading his invisible audience in prayer. Esther's eyes were
dog eyes, cow eyes, baleful, uncomprehending, while in-
ward worlds revolved in silence. She rubbed her hands on
her apron, saying *See sill* abstractly, without volition like
an instrument used to project another's voice.

    It followed him up the stairs. That Cecil from her lips a
shadow as he climbed to the second floor. *See sill.* They all
answered to his name, those ghosts he felt each morning
slipping into his clothes as he dressed. It was their presence
which sustained him, but in November they grew dark and
heavy like leaves he needed desperately to shed. Clinging
leaves, dead leaves which killed before they fell. It was a
pattern, a cycle he had been aware of for years. The ghosts
were part of him, his energy revived them, fleshed them,
and in turn they hid his nakedness. Then November. Lead

skies which leaned but not heavily enough, earth which sucked greedily but would not jerk them down. Autumn when each one took a day to fall, and in its fall was a sliver of his flesh screaming till it touched the ground.

She wouldn't know his name. The red-haired woman could say *Cecil,* could add another ghost, but she wouldn't know his name. He asked himself why not keep walking, why not up past these tithes on one and two and knock at her door. She would have to answer or not. And if she answered, she could only say go away or yes come in. All the uncertainty, the fears, would resolve themselves into a series of simple choices. No gods involved, no turnings of the earth. Just her very human responses, unpredictable but within a limited, unspectacular range. She is afterall only a woman, one who has reached thirty or thereabouts through a course of trial and error, a course in which my intrusion would be assimilated like all other events, growing smaller in significance as it is succeeded by other events, other states of mind. If she is an intelligent woman, she knows all this, she knows my wish to touch, to help, even to hurt, is much greater than any capacity I have to change her. If she knows, the door should . . . but it is November and there is dying to do. I will not knock.

But she is there. A white blur leaning over the banister. Is it her voice or do I smell her, taste her, touch her in the dark stairwell.

Why did you do it. This time he is caught; he must answer. So much red on the pillow, soft red he can smooth or tangle in his fist. He should be brave. The flesh of her he can bathe in as he pleases. The sleep-snow whiteness in which he can ink deeply the heat of his hands, foot or lips. S. Sherman has been waiting for thirty-two years. Not for Cecil, not in maiden lust for the buck janitor who wanders in her dreams, but waiting for that time when need says take a man for the flesh, release the body from its bondage

7

to the phantoms who think they rule and thinking rule. Let a man come to you though his hands stink and you don't know him.

Cecil had hoped it would be red too. That patch of matting unruly over her cleft. But auburn curls around his fingers, the color of freckles between her breasts. Esther's was a hedge you had to crawl through before the meadow spread sunlit and swaying, but these feathers or a tongue tickling almost. I remember once I asked Esther not to move and my ear was on the bush and I listened inside her till we went to sleep. That was early when we believed and there was some point in stopping and listening. There is no point now asking me *why*. Man who threw can plunged with it and cracked his crockery head on concrete. Might as well ask why I died inside her. Why I trembled once, and all man in me ran out like a little boy from a dark room. Can was a bedbug I found in my shirt. Can was the breakfast Esther didn't cook. Can was what I crumpled because I have a hand and because I like to know hand can crumple.

Esther now. There are wheels and they turn and they move her but they are not her wheels. At most perhaps Esther hears chug, chug of washing machine in the basement. Who painted her name on the mailbox. Did the painter know what the initial stood for? May I ask?

Got up the goddamn stairs pretty quick. I don't think anybody saw me go in. Her apartment on the end. Woman turns on her side now, draws her knees toward her chest. Cecil's head on high pillow of her hip. There is nothing in the glance they exchange. A door slamming, footsteps in the hall, and they can smile, his hand can go to her cheek, she can roll languidly on her back.

Esther said she was staying home, a horrible headache, and she had already called them and told them she wouldn't be in. It was strange that she didn't really know. November and the dying. All these years and neither told nor did she ask. She knew he spent days in bed, that he shut off his bedroom from the rest of the apartment and warned Esther and her aunt not to disturb him. She knew certain times were worse than others and perhaps intuitively dreaded the coming of fall and his *moods* as she called them, but rather than look for some pattern, she chose to believe her periods of worried anticipation arose from some soul link between her and her husband. She believed their life together had been preordained by an all powerful force, and since this source was God in heaven, the joining of their lives had to be right no matter how far this rightness might be submerged beneath the troubled surface of their days together. Only after a prolonged battle with herself had she come to realize how God had blessed her. That He had blessed her with a trial. Cecil would be her salvation, her road to humility, the means through which she would finally be placed beside her Creator.

There was a finality, a fatality in it all. Even her Aunt Fanny, coming when she did, that last year when Cecil lived at the law school, fit into the picture, which was now consummately clear. Esther had blamed the old woman, cursed her for giving Cecil an excuse to make the last move from their bed into the dormitory room, where he slept alone. But God made Esther see why Cecil had to move and how in His compassion He had foreseen all and sent Aunt Fanny to take the place of the man she could no longer have.

So much cleaning to be done. One load of clothes up and drying, another in the machine, and still a stack by the door waiting its turn. When everything clean, the ironing to do, then the four untidy rooms in which she felt no one but she lifted a finger to keep clean. Sometimes over the ironing board her headaches seemed to get better. Her arms would move slowly and her fingers grip the warm, black handle.

She could go as slowly as she wanted in and out of the folds of material, pressing, creasing; she could take her coffee and listen to the radio played softly. Gospels if she could find them and best when the slow, sad ones she could sway her whole body to as the iron glided and hissed. She could forget the white heat in the left half of her brain, she could swallow the scream that squirmed behind her teeth, she could deny the damp palms of her hands which ached for the lacerating kiss of clenched fist and fingernails biting deep. It was dancing at the Horizon Room I believe Cecil first said he could feel me hot down there, heat of me coming through my clothes and his clothes. He never said love but he said Esther you are better than you know. You would smile more if you knew the secrets you know. What he said was enough and I couldn't say no I closed my eyes and did it and I hoped in time he would say the rest.

In one corner a rectangle of light trembled on the concrete floor. The patch of light caught the delicate, twisting shadow of the atmosphere—the mobile dust motes and hissing furnace breath—which played across the small window flush with the basement ceiling. Since this window was the only one in the basement and Cecil hadn't replaced the dead bulb outside the rear of their apartment, Esther, her arms filled by a clothes hamper, clothespins, and a box of detergent, had to pick her way through darkness to the laundry room. Though she had made the trip thousands of times and with armloads more precarious than what encumbered her at the moment, Esther cautiously inched her way across the rough floor. She was afraid of falling. Her blood warned her that the fall might never end, that floor and earth would give way, that there were unimaginable distances to plummet through forever. It galled her that Cecil moved easily in this darkness, that with a cat's eyes and feet he could go anywhere he wanted without bumping things or tripping. Even when he was drunk and had just about fallen

10

down the last flight of stairs into the basement, once his feet touched the concrete, his movements would be sober, efficient. The cool, dark air seemed to restore him, to right a balance; he was a fish who had recovered its element, who could stop the frantic writhing of his moment on the sand.

The pain in her head was crisp now, a bell distinct and deliberate, giving form to the hours. It was better this way. Pain just before sleep or pain born with consciousness in the morning was blurred, distorted into *always has been and will be* because pain leaned on the unknown, shared its boundaries with unfathomable stretches of not quite real, of a kind of death. The brain could not focus, could not say where pain came from or where it might lead. Whispers said there is only pain and dream, dream and pain. Esther's feet slid lightly across the coarse grain of the concrete, but the sound grated upon the fibers of her brain. Cecil had killed the rats, but she felt that any moment a squirming, melon softness would give way beneath her feet and the fall begin. Monotonous, ungentle churning of the washing machine seemed to contain a message of assurance; the arc of light around the laundry room door was a sanctuary where all would be fine. One foot then the other pushed forward, toes straining through bottoms of thin slippers to feel their way, test the substance on which everything depended. Night in a strange house on a high, unlighted landing trying to find where the stairs begin. It wasn't far to the laundry room, but how long had she been edging her way on this narrow ridge above the abyss. How long wind chewing the insides of her skull. She lurches through the door, the basket squeals and pushes against her bosom when it is flung upon the high green table and her whole weight collapses on its woven frame.

Footsteps bird quick and light. Little Aunt Fanny hurries from her nest in the home of Cecil Braithwaite to the laundry room where Esther waits strength to pray away her pain.

Aunt Fanny tiny in the doorway, so frail, unreal, she could be a creature of Esther's pain dream, and for a second Esther believes she can think it away, if not the complete dream at least this one transparent image shooed away with an effort of will. But Fanny speaks, brittle, high-pitched like the records that play inside talking dolls.

–Do you want me to help. Do you want me to help. Always like that, twice quick in succession she would nervously repeat a simple phrase as if to assure the hearer that she had spoken, that she could speak. Esther knew her hands were shaking. She buried them in the hamper of soiled laundry. The thought and action were swift, almost a reflex to sudden apparition of old woman in the doorway. Even so, the instant that elapsed made speaking to her aunt possible. Because she couldn't trust its firmness at a lower tone, Esther's voice was too loud in the small room.

–You go back, Fanny. I'm almost finished here. You get your rest. Fanny didn't reply she didn't say I just got up out of bed and don't need or want rest didn't say I came to speak to you to hear myself talking or hear you speak didn't say please, please or weep or stamp her tiny foot she said nothing just twirled her hands at her waist in two tight, rapid circles and nearly smiling walked away.

Eggs boiling in a small pan on a too high flame can make the sound of an angry sea. It must be Fanny at the stove, Fanny whom I've never seen eat other than boiled eggs. Lives on eggs and coffee little old woman under this roof with me. Who am I? Cecil Otis Braithwaite, born October 2, 1933, in the District of Columbia. Suffered under various pilots till earning my own wings ascended to the summit of the law, where it was my job to speak for those about to be judged. Lawyer Braithwaite, third of his race to be admitted and second to finish the university law school aided and abetted throughout by unflagging efforts of Esther Brown, true avatar of that selfless, sore-kneed mother every night scrubbing the halls bright so next morning second generation son could tall stride the shining corridors. Esther on all fours, the solid rock on which I stood *cum laude*. Esther funeral flower weary in the rear of the huge auditorium as pomp and circumstance led me down the aisle, then flower plucked, leaning on my arm second time in the same day down another aisle wedding march we do. On the side of the bed later that night I remember sitting and listening to the clock. Everything before me. Even Fanny gone for a honeymoon week. A new place of our own soon. I sat so long Esther fell asleep; it was no wonder eight years opening those doors it was enough for her to fall through exhausted when entrance finally made. Black pants baggy about the knees and million furrows across back of jacket, they hung limp, suspenders dangling from same hanger on the door hook. I in my T-shirt and shorts sat so long I was stiff when at last I had to move. Eight years but now those two trips down carpeted aisles made everything all right, all right.

It was a beautiful day and they said if life did not begin full, rich, I had only myself to blame. The others liked me as much as they could. Cecil a piece of their education, something to be coped with, to come to terms with, a measure of their powers of self-control, of their intellect's flexibility. They were successful on the whole. Only a few times did they forget, did the eyes in a body turn on me or away. The best is not wasted on Cecil. From the back, from a distance you can hardly tell. Together in our black robes and mortar boards you had to be looking to find him in the class picture. Old Cec. It's not that we don't want him to come, we don't ask him because we know he doesn't want to come; we know he has his own way to go, his own people, his own woman, he is in love.

I heard or perhaps dreamed Esther moving about, the waterfall, her hand finally on my shoulder *come on my sleepy-head baby* I believe I heard it all but kept my eyes shut tight and rolled away from touch from sounds. I'm not so sure about the crying. Dream or Esther when I opened my eyes. She was beside me curled in her robe. The sealed fastness of the robe, the inert mass of her covered flesh I could not go to, could not disturb as I sat awake needing what should be beneath the blue corduroy.

The suit slithered from the door and I was covered and in the street. I saw her no more for three years.

Dear Esther,

You will not read this. You could not read this if some miracle caused these words to appear on a sheet of paper in your lap. Weeks have passed and only notes from me to say I need this or that, five dollars at a post office in a city far from you, money I never wait for or catch. I have assured you that I am healthy and sane that you had done nothing wrong and that you could only wait, just as I was waiting. When I left, I simply left. No destination, no intention, just a move to the other side of the door. I thought for a moment I wanted to see the stars, walk as I often did in the quiet of night alone. Nothing seemed to be on my mind. The moment, and it has been the same moment ever since, carried me with it, drained time of all meaning. I was confused even alarmed when I realized my sense of time, of myself in time had ceased to function, not simply blurred or distorted but blotted out completely as light from a blind man's eyes. Like a man suddenly blind there was panic in my first gropings; I had no means of control, of balance or direction. But more quickly than you would imagine, other senses began to assert themselves, a driving necessity to move, to go on, itself became not only the end but the means of propelling myself through a strange world. I wanted to giggle at the moon. I wanted to run and watch it trying to catch me over the rooftops.

I was afraid I was out too late, that I would be scolded, even beaten if I didn't hurry home. I made up excuses. I began to recall all the demons I'd grown up with. The streets shrank, narrower, darker and I smelled the rot of garbage, of derelict cars, of winos whose outstretched feet you had to step over to get past the corner. But that was only one world. You were there too, Esther. Your door was one of those calling me, one to which I was returning as soon as the moment passed, the moment when all the worlds were equal, each cluttering my vision of the others so I couldn't move, could only wait for some *now* to return.

If someone asked me the date I would look at a mirror, if someone asked me who I was I would want to see a calendar. I won't be asking you for anything else. If this is a bubble, it will burst and when it does I will know and you will know. I know it is not fair to reach back, to lie to you and say there is this much Cecil remaining, this much of him unchanged because he assumes certain rights, perpetuates obligations. I will not write again, not even send this. The black warrior told her fabulous lies. Told her of islands in the sky, men with heads beneath their shoulders. He did not tell her he still searched, that she was the unvisited land he would explore, that he would conquer deftly but with dread, his thick hands peeling one by one layers of silk from her thighs.

The librarian handed him the large, heavy book. St. Veronica was in the center of the glossy dust jacket, a Veronica self-absorbed, palely tranquil against a background of ruddy demonic faces, St. Veronica, whose long, clean forehead and heavy nose gave her face in profile a downward thrust, a kind of humility that pushed her chin against her slender neck, even pulled down the lids of her browless eyes, a face that could be masculine in its unsubtle, almost coarse features, yet a face that absorbed light into its skin, that emphasized the tentativeness, the transparency of the flesh and the fragility of bones beneath, St. Veronica's face utterly submissive yet removed from all the turbulence surrounding her, from the accident of His murder, benign,

15

dreaming His image on the sudarium, loving the relic while the man still breathes and bleeds, Veronica's face in its sublime indifference so startlingly and simply Esther's face.

The work of Hieronymus Bosch has fascinated and disturbed men from his own time down to today. Born in the middle of the fifteenth century . . . Cecil read only this far. He leafed through the illustrations of Bosch's paintings looking for Veronica's face, for Esther's face to be repeated. He also searched for the black men in Bosch. The Negroes were there, they had to be there and in many forms and roles. The Magus, the waiter at the Black Mass, initiates male and female in the Garden, a mason raising the towers of Hell. Cecil found other saints' faces, saints beset, saints despairing, edified, penitent, musing and passive saints, but no face like that of Veronica, no saint's features and expression that said I am waiting, I have this much of you and I am content to wait.

Cecil's face settled onto the spread-eagled pillow of the big book. He sat alone at a table in the rear of the reading room, with his back toward the chief librarian's desk. Back and forth between them two fans cut high in the paneled walls shuttled the heavy air. They were bothersome flies then bees peacefully droning Cecil to sleep in a glade of tall, swaying grass. His corner had the restful gloom of all library corners and the book could have been a convenient headstone in a rural cemetery where all the dead had welcomed him. Miss Pruitt was not quite dead nor did she welcome Cecil. She called Anisse, her assistant, the girl who had given Cecil his book.

–That colored man over there, Miss Johnson, the one in the dark suit asleep. Either he must read or go away. There are park benches more suitable for what he wants to do. Please inform him of the rules of our library.

–Sir, sir. . . . Cecil looked into the squirrel face, the soft eyes, and small lips barely parted whispering.

16

–Sir, you'll have to wake up or leave. Miss Pruitt sent me over so I think you'd better listen, sir.

–You wouldn't mind if I stayed.

–She wouldn't mind either if you follow the rules, sir.

–But you, I mean would you care if I read or not.

–To be quite honest, no, I wouldn't care. It's a big, nearly empty room, and I don't see why I should care. Or anyone care.

–Then I'll stay.

–But only if you read.

Mirror said time was Cecil when you could not see your face unless someone lifted you to broken glass above the sink. Later you didn't care about image just run, run all day stopping only when tired and maybe seeing dim shadows in a puddle or on the drenched pavement, then one day saw woolly hair and dust that wouldn't wash off you saw colored boy Cecil and really surprised you saw something you had no way of knowing different or worse you saw your face and knew the dust would not change and now you see all things go away but that doesn't go away woolly hair creeps back on your forehead, but only reveals more dust beneath you will always be dying Cecil but that will not die. Cecil's hands rubbed hot then cold water into his face. The library's washroom was the cleanest he'd been in for days, and its cleanliness enabled him to try and tidy his person, to wash, to comb, to straighten the bedraggled clothing on his body as best he could. It seemed proper here in this neat washroom, a possibility that the other foul-smelling ill-lighted jakes had made inconceivable. He wondered why he hadn't thought of libraries before. Perhaps they were rooted too deeply in the other element—books and silent cubicles, alcoves stale with page dust and nervous, muffled breathing as word kindled in dry heatless extinction. Word become flesh become Cecil become invisible opener of doors, lightener of burden, of care, of pigmentation even, transforming mirror Cecil to that which only if you try hard can you find between black parenthesis of mortar board and gown.

Cecil shit and washed his hands again. She had been wearing a loose, green dress, the one who came and spoke to him, who had soft eyes. It could have been a tenuous rapport he sensed or just the ambiguity of his own half-sleep that suffused an aura of intimacy over the conversation. He had asked her name. She was a stranger, but less so than the others. Her green dress.

I should have asked her, Cecil thought, what city this is, what day of the month, of what year. Hearing from her would be somehow appropriate. I know she would tell me what I asked, no more, no less, and that she would tell the truth as far as she was able if I asked her other questions, if I made more demands. Her voice blending with rustle of green dress, perfume. Green color of St. Barbara's dress. Her symbol a tower. I remember a drawing, Eyckian perhaps, in which behind the saint men are erecting (delicately delineated by the artist, bare ribs of tentative form) her tower. Her dress spreads, a lush growing thing, on the hillside, and she gazes up from a book, quill in hand. The workmen, the saint, all motion and activity of the scene arrested, classically static and yet clearly projecting the shape and necessity of their completion like the tower rising from its chrysalis of scaffolding.

Cecil does not see her again. Shadows deepen and the fire goes out behind panes of stained glass. He would have preferred music, but the big books of old pictures had nearly the same soothing effect, emptied him into oblivion.

He saw her framed in the yellow rectangle, naked, not giving a fuck, guzzling whisky from a bottle. Life's done this to me she said and life is your eyes taking me in. All naked pink of me, pot-bellied, saggy titted, clump of hair there and here under my arm as I raise this bottle and don't

18

give a fuck who knows or sees. Window yellow and shade-
less, an eye that can't look away, can't blink or shield itself
with a tear. Naked lady in the window. Who do you love;
who has loved you. Would anyone pinch your melting backside, grin at you. She drinks. It will be morning soon, even
now somewhere the light is scratching out someone's eyes.
He wonders if the whisky still goes down, if it still spreads
and tickles inside the pink flesh. He cannot remember a
night that has been different. He has been always walking
black, empty streets, streets on which every walker is alone,
enclosed in the echo of his own footfalls. Dirty streets even
in the blackness, and windows that brush his shoulders. The
naked woman drinks, a flesh pillow round her middle, tired
breasts that drag, the scraggly beard. Did she see him; he
could have touched her, thrust his hand in the yellow frame
if the glass had vanished. It was always her street, their
street, and he the interloper, the one who is given away by
his loud footsteps, his heart beating.

Cecil knew he would see her again. As he approached a
rare lighted window each time he thought she would be
there again. Something moved her in endless visitations
through the rooms of the narrow row houses just as it
moved him along the black pavement that was a ribbon
around them. She was the fat, pink owner and the exploited
tenant just as Cecil was the echo and the sound of his night
wanderings. No one had wed them, no one had even intro-
duced them and yet they were blind lovers eternally bound.
Cecil and the lady, Cecil sound and Cecil echo, landlord
and tenant.

And the street curved and rose and fell and hugged its
shadow to itself and became all glass and winking light and
slept again and almost died and finally like blood going
home emptied into a loud, bright sea. Cecil emerging took
the broad perpendicular—Market Street—and walked toward the city's center. After crossing a bridge he turned off

into the railroad station. To a congregation of taxicabs and travelers a recorded voice squawked instructions. Yellow tickees for yellow cabs were automatically ejaculated from a blunt snouted machine beside the double revolving doors of the station's entrance. Alms for the love of Allah Cecil thought he heard and reached out to take a yellow ticket. It was freshly stamped: time, date, and serial number. The parrot urged him to take another, for anyone going anywhere to take another and go the best, fastest way. Cecil watched a long, gracefully curved leg slowly draw itself into the back seat of a cab. The beautiful face smiled at the black driver and told him swiftly where it wanted to go. In a moment they were disappearing together into the night.

And after the beginning the end, and after the rise the fall, and after Cecil the calm scalloped breath of a fart entered the Thirtieth Street station. A Family that Strays Together, Stays Together. Buy Bonds, They Did. A Name You Can Trust.

Its always a god they wait for. They wait because they believe, because they have faith. Not many inside at this hour. Sprawled on benches, eating, reading at the snack-magazine counter. Your people wheeling scrub buckets; some even command mopping machines. Someday there will be robots for the job and your people eating or reading or waiting to go.

Somebody was coming home. Somebody cocooned in rich, dark wood. Cecil shuffled across the cold stones of the station floor looking neither to the right nor the left, not down at his unlaced shoes nor up at the distant vault of the ceiling. Cecil obeyed and did not look back, he was to become no salt pillar, no last minute loser of his love, no food for rocks on which the women sat singing. His course was clear. Night waited opposite the door he had entered, night and the group in black beside black limousines. The mourners had been too punctual. They had to watch the cheap pine slats stripped away, the friction build between the mortician's immaculate staff and the coveralled Railway Express men. The shell of yellow boards had no sorrow in them. They split, squealed, and giggled like spring girls being undone. Finally the coffin sat ornate and gleaming under the electric lights that studded the overhang of the baggage porch. The coffin was already a thing detached, mute, indifferent, secure in its order of time. Not the time of the mourners (perhaps mother, father, brother, and wife, perhaps children and grandchildren, perhaps not blood at all but brought by some other coincidence to wait for the train), but the sea time of ebb and flow, of change faceless and forever renewing. Cecil saw there were tears. And the old man with his arm around the thin shoulders of the old veiled woman. The fingers did not stretch themselves upon her flesh. Long, dry hand hung limp against the breast of her black dress, knobby bones touching one another, an animal the woman could be wearing as decoration. It was lifted ever so gently, the polished coffin, which if shrunken would have served as an elegant jewel box for a lady's vanity table. Behind the old couple, young woman and man, other Negroes dressed in black stood at hushed attention. Cecil knew they would soon begin to sing.

Cecil thought the moment had created its own kind of sepulchral silence, a threshold of quiet until the box was in the hearse and the dearly beloved who had gathered could sing it away. But the city found their corner. Cars, trains, buses, the loudspeaker hoarse with the stationmaster's voice, porters calling, newspapers hawked, it all came crowding into the small, quiet place beneath the overhang. Cecil remembered a blind shooting up, the rattling echo of its violent motion that shook the tiny, rented cubicle where he and Esther lay. Surprise, surprise they all said as one after another climbed through the sudden hole in the wall. Cossacks, traveling salesmen, senators, whores, football

21

players, a baboon, a steel drum band poured through smiling and excited. He bolted upright in the unsteady cot. The guests were a flood inundating the room, water rising to his chin. Beside him she was already dead, drowned, the twisted sheet shrouding her lifeless flesh. Light choked him, chewed his scream. . . .

> Farther along we'll know more about you,
> Farther along we'll understand why.
> I want you to cheer up, my brethren,
> Live in the sunshine.
> You'll understand—
> By and by. . . .

Why did you do it. This time he is caught, he must answer. So much red on the pillow, soft red he can smooth or tangle in his fist. Can I tell her Simon is dead, my son Simon out of Esther who has our underwear already up and drying whom I have had to refuse once already this morning. Simon conceived in November, born dead in spring. Simon is why I killed what was in my hands why they grin when I pass. You must hear them laughing, the bags of garbage mocking humped Cecil as he descends the back stairs. You see it has not always been like this. You might laugh too if I produced the diploma, think it was something I bought at a rummage sale or scavenged from the bags. You don't know my name. You might believe I took my name from the document I found, took his name as I took his degree and nailed it to my wall. Hocus-pocus. Let there be Cecil. Because if you are Cecil and you are what it says on the paper then who is crazy nigger I know playing on these back stairs, making noise that breaks people's sleep.

For a somnambulist she moves faster than you'd expect.

22

Quickly she is down there at my root taking back her own, the loam returned to her lips that I dredged from her lips. Perfect circle. And should I be Indian giver too. Succubus curled at the gate waiting for rain.

Teeth and hair. Immaculate conception recorded three times in this century produced just that, a growth of hair and teeth. Perhaps preserved somewhere in a jar. My Simon nowhere, a dead son not rare at all, to be expected, even predictable, out of a thousand births, two hundred babies will not get past the first month. But I did not have a thousand sons; I tempted the number gods in no way. In fact I tried to be humble, wanted only one son, waited once for one son. Loved all that Esther and I had done together, all we would ever do. So when he came and died so soon . . . So when he came and died so soon . . .

There is a window. From where I rest my head on her breasts I can look through a three-sided window made by her splayed raised thighs and lintel of calf, ankle, and foot crossing them. I can see Simon building a house of alphabet blocks. I can see Simon mashing crayons on a coloring book. I can see Esther washing Simon and me washing Esther and the three of us laughing and splashing naked in the soapy water. The lintel drops, and there is only wide V of two white thighs pointing toward the ceiling.

I will go with him to the park. There will be peacocks strutting unexpected at the sudden turnings of wooded paths, a fountain and a wide basin around it for sailing miniature boats. Simon's boat will lean into the wind, a gleaming scimitar, a swan. I will watch it glide, watch him, grow drowsy in the afternoon sun. I will doze till Simon shakes my knee.

—It was naughty what you did. I'm sure others must have heard the racket. Cecil combed the redness with his fingers. Her hair had become wet and tangled, but as Cecil drew his hand in long gentle strokes smoothness and lightness

23

returned. As if moved by a puff of air a few wisps of red responding to some energy in his hand would rise after each stroke. A kind of magic Cecil thought. You rub your feet on a rug then touch a metal doorknob and a spark crackles. A comb through your hair and it makes tissue paper stick. Cecil waved his hand above the redness. Silky strands strained to reach him. Moon above the tides of a red sea. Cecil's game as he did not answer, as he listened, as he searched for more windows, mirrors, eyes.

–I've never done anything like this before, she said. Cecil thought how everything would have been the first time for Simon, how many *first times* Simon would never have. Why. Cecil wondered if anything like bad luck in November could be passed from generation to generation, if the blood could carry images of dying leaves, still, dark pools, a thousand fleeing wings, if all the sadness of fall sky and earth could be reborn in Simon's heart. What had the child learned in that less than one instant of life. And did Simon learn or did Simon simply have to remember.

–Oh Cecil, if it could have just been me. If I could just take his place. Esther seemed to have dissolved into grief; she was not the lump in the hospital gown and bed, but part of the dense atmosphere, the disinfectant and blood pall which burned Cecil's eyes and nose in the crowded maternity ward.

–Of course I knew a thing like this could happen, might happen to me. But the picture, vague as it was, was somehow quite different from this. When I was a girl, I . . .

–Why Simon, Cecil? Somebody you know named Simon, somebody in your family. You mean like Simon Peter in the Bible? Sounds kind of strange to me. I'm not sure as I like it. No sense in worrying now anyway. Just as easy be a girl. · · ·

As my son died her red hair keeps falling. It is sand through my fingers. Here I lie with this strange white

24

woman and Esther downstairs and Simon dead. She asks *why did you do it.*

All I could think of was Easter and the way all the choirs were singing. You see when you try to answer a question such things come up. My wife and her spirituals. A bunch of us had a group and used to sing. Everything from rhythm and blues to gospels which is not as far you'd think till you've heard a lot of them, then no question of shared roots. Still you know precisely what the good ones want to say. No question about it. In the gospels they are saying I believe and this is the way it is to feel like I do. Easter was old Reverend Reed, but it had to accommodate the song of Schütz as well. Reverend Reed and beside and beneath him on a straight-backed chair Mr. Watkins who was not Reverend because he could not read or write, an ignorant, country black man fast becoming child again as years collapsed the bones of his face, the bones of his sleeping intellect. I saw him on the street long after those days when with Esther I would go to hear the singing and try to make out what words moved Esther's lips as she silently prayed. He was there, Elder Watkins his title at last, Elder Watkins in the remains of a blue vested suit. He still wore the heavy gold chain looped from his watch pocket and the tall black hat with drooping brim. I knew if I had been closer I would have smelled the age, the weariness of flesh and threadbare fabric. Of the million lines that sliced across the Elder's face, I remember those at the corners of his eyes, eyes that seemed forgotten under folds of skin. These lines intaglioed black against dusky black at the outward corners of his eyes could have been the beginnings of a smile. The good Elder Watkins. I could see the frayed ends of long cotton drawers below the blue trousers. The same gray-white cotton showed through rents in the old man's shoes as he shuffled through Casino Way, a loaf of bread under his arm. Good day Elder. Did you know they are singing again, Easter song Elder, by a German you should have known, Heinrich Schütz, who would surely recognize that Jesus shuffle of yours beneath a cross of dignity here in a back alley bringing home the bacon. Man . . . man, do you hear me talking to you. Why will you die, sink down onto the pavement when I turn away? The Elder was on his knees, his hands were clasped and sweat poured down his face in the effort of maintaining with dignity the uncomfortable posture and recalling those sacred cadences, seeking and finding the rhythm that would make the words flow, which would swing that rusty gate of memory back and let the word roam green pastures. It was all there. In the black head sprinkled with salt and pepper tufts of hair. He had learned it all by listening. He was a vessel into which the word had been poured. And if he pressed his knees into the hard boards of the altar platform and strained the muscles of his old neck to hold the head back and eyeballs fixed on Heaven, then the gate would glide back. So I had listened to the old man babble on. Cento of biblical fragments, of scripture, hymns and favorite phrases of all the Reverends he had served beneath. And there were days the Elder found his poetry. The sun shone while rain fell. Devil beating his wife, and Esther of course cried when Reverend Reed thundered over the Elder's prayer, when poor Elder Watkins got carried away and floundered in those deep waters, when his tongue clucked and we all feared now it's the old man's time his heart can't bear these memories, this song that makes him tremble and sweat and stutter, but he didn't die just faded away under Reverend Reed's thunder from the pulpit. And here the Elder was. Like a blind man making his way through this alley. That alley where I wanted to speak, to say Elder I remember you, you are not dead yet, not a ghost yet though you could be the tattered shade of a black Polonius, of ignorance and desperate dignity done to death like a rat.

But I did not disturb him. I went on my way to the Presbyterian church and heard the St. John Passion of Schütz. I believe these things happened the same day . . . Easter . . .

–When I was a girl I hated the freckles and the red hair was just as bad. Somehow they went together. It was *them* that made me ugly. One day if I could just be patient, they would go away and ugly duckling be a swan. A blond swan with clear white skin. She rose and stood beside the bed. Cecil remaining on the bed got up to his knees and pulled her toward him till his arms were tight around the firm, powerful middle of the woman. Strong bones, tight flesh of hips and taut lower belly. Cecil diver plunged into the perfumed depths of her body hair still damp from their lovemaking. His fingers dug into her haunches, spreading and closing the two massy petals of her backside. She moaned, then the moan was a flower blooming, a thrust of naked beauty that was a liquid tongue meeting Cecil's, licking Cecil's, washing Cecil, floating him as seed to the hot inner chambers of his own desire.

And while the tongue was swallowed, another formed in the forest.

Christ lag in Todesbanden. That was another Easter. And Easter in Spain, in Madrid, in Málaga, how many times has the body been resurrected in his name. *Schlafe, schlafe mein Liebster.* Sleep Simon.

And I wanted love so badly I dreamed of encounters under rocks, in the sea slime. My search has brought me here to this white woman's bed, to the aftertaste of her juices in my mouth. If I called Esther at the top of my voice, she might hear me through the three floors and run here to claim me, to take me back below the stairs where she knows I belong.

The room is silent, naked man and woman prostrate in postures of exhaustion. The room shook to the chugging of the washing machine. The room was hung with the damp skins of dead animals. In the room both beds were unmade

27

and a small yellow woman in a rocking chair twirled her hands. The room was empty now, the stacks of clothes removed and Esther on her way through the darkness.

So many things Esther didn't know. Cecil counted, one, two, three . . . on his graduation eve, half enjoying, half dismayed by his secrets. Herbert Philbrick, F.B.I. double agent, led three lives each week on TV in a perpetual turning of tables upon the communist conspiracy. Cecil had been bored by the show but identified with the numbers compartmentalizing the double agent's lives. Cecil defender of the faith: lover of Esther, diligent student of the law, advancer of banner proclaiming *All Men Equal.* Cecil conspirator: lover of love, student of *their* law, carrot wiggled in front of the others *Equal Opportunity Lives.* Cecil Cecil: neither of others, libra, seesaw, see soul, sees all.

Home for a haircut. Sometimes leaving the law school building and university grounds took on an urgency, a one-track necessity like the stinging need to urinate or lose his seed. Today going through the mechanics of his final leave-taking there had been no wistfulness. He had read the instruction sheet and efficiently carried out his tasks. No one had been in the superintendent's office when Cecil had replaced his key on the appropriate hook. Number 203. The last year he had lived among them on the campus rather than with Esther. That was part of his scholarship, a condition which had annoyed him, but which he couldn't afford to refuse. It meant evening and weekend safaris to catch up on his janitorial duties at the Banbury Arms. It meant Esther doing much of his job in addition to her own. He had not told her that the move away had meant his bills would be paid. Instead he continued to collect the money she had

28

been supplying throughout his career in law school. To surprise her with what she would never buy for herself, some gift, some extravagance? Or was it originally for a child? Whatever his intent, his initial reason for secrecy, he scrupulously hoarded Esther's savings.

Someone whom he would probably never see again, unless they bumped in the pomp and circumstance parade tomorrow, had lent Cecil the money for a haircut, and though it was a long way, Cecil had set out on foot for the barber's.

As usual June was hot and got hotter as Cecil got closer to home. Everybody knows how it is now thought Cecil. Information abounds about us down here just as it does about those over there and *that kind* and *them*. We have been measured, quantified by tools so subtle that they tell better lies than most men. And what is the ritual in dying. Does my number when it's up drop or jerk or is it drawn through by a black pencil. And in that room where all our cards are filed does some lugubrious arm in a solemn arc glide over the metal trays till it comes to B then Br then Bra and so on till it has located one Braithwaite, Cecil Otis, then delicately descend, clamp my card in its pincers, raise me, retrace the arc backward till I am suspended over the proper heap of other numbers up. Drops me. Or is there an afterlife, some limbo cabinet in which are housed defunct numbers for a decent interval, for a storage bin repose while all cross references are checked out: tardy credits, overdue accounts, invoices, actions, loans, liens, disposition of estates all are collected, balanced. Books on everything. Why my manhood measures less than it should. Something to do with being lost when I was found, with being made to dance so my legs would not wither, dancing to a cat-o'-nine-tails, with being made to watch and listen while my women did other dances with the sailors. I remember the sun sudden in my eyes, the salt air too rich after the fetid hole below decks. Music began cracking around me and though it tore

29

my ankles and drew flies to the bloody ankle chains, I jiggled my body to make it live another day, to be raised another day to sun and salt air and flagellation.

If I were to write a book it would have no numbers. Sick of Numbers Cecil said almost aloud.

How you doing Magistrate Cecil. The voice and greeting told him he was getting closer and closer. Up from the broken pavement rose the wavering heat. I believe the women wear pants instead of skirts just so they can sit with their legs wide open. She smiled at him from three stories up, toothless witch, her bones held together by an ancient cotton dress; bare throat, bare brown shoulders, she had been waiting for golden hair to grow, to drop into the street, for some knight to climb and release her, but now she had forgotten, only smiled at what passed, even sweaty, haircut needing Cecil below her window she would acknowledge as she did the buses, the dogs and cats, the beer, the grease. Their sea changed forms which dried where they splattered Rorschach blots of I am going nowhere so might as well be here against this building or let it fall where it will right here in the middle of the sidewalk I ain't going nowhere and couldn't care less. Or I am sick.

Handkerchief across his brow, Cecil paused in the midst of the mopping strokes to finger the tight curls of his longer than necessary hair. *What's to it, Magistrate.* To be well groomed essential. An incipient pun in the word groom, its double meaning in relation to Esther and their wedding the next day fixed the word groom in Cecil's mind. Groom, gloom, gloam, gleem, groom, loom, broom, poom. Do you undertake this womb to be your lawful wedded wife. The room was full of men and women attired in black. Some laughed, some cried, others moved among the floral decorations with no expression of emotion on their faces. Black watch. Soon a door would be opened and the mystery would recede. Pipers piping. Gloom pipes. Down from heel and hills pied piper and plague of worms. Bitches hide wombs. Batches fried grooms. The building you see before you is all that remains of the ancient ghetto. We have conjectured from drawings on its walls and instruments petrified in the lava flow that this edifice served as a house of pleasure. Sociopologists have recently discovered municipal records which seem to point to the existence of an extensive number of these bordellos in this area suggesting that perhaps one of the thriving industries of the ghetto was prostitution. No one can accurately estimate what percentage of its residents actually lived from the profits of that profession, and of course there remains the problem of determining primary and secondary participation but modern methods of research and data evaluation are everyday opening up to us the secrets of this lost culture. I wish to call your special attention to the rounded groove in this stone. We have reason to believe that the contour was not carved nor is it a freak of nature, rather we suppose it was worn by the buttocks of long dead ladies of the night who for as closely as we can guess spent thousands of years in this very spot waiting for their male customers.

Sick and desolate of an old passion.

Shine, shine, shine
Shine for a nickel
Shine for a dime
Shine for a quarter
If you got the time.

Boy sang to Cecil, to the sun. Litany of the old street. One-eyed boy with box tucked under his arm, shoeshine rags draped over his left shoulder next to the good eye. He would shine, shine. Better than the sun he would pop and flick and rub till grinning back from the toe of a boot his face would appear. Two-faced. Two good eyes. Boy past, boy future Cecil glanced at the scarred toes of his shoes, the visible coats of liquid polish thinly glazing one another and never reaching the leather somewhere brown and dying beneath. I would my fingers held some musical instrument—a guitar, a fiddle. I would play beside the boy, accompany him along the street. And each time we stopped to emblazon some customer a crowd would gather, watch him pop and flick and rub and they would hear how all this, these smells, the filth, the sweat, *How you doing Magistrate* has not been lost, does not tremble away like hot sidewalks or die like the scream of the siren but lights a corner in a man, a dark huddling corner but one which lives until the next burst of sun or salt air too rich.

Pearl that was his eye. Pearly ball dimmed by the writhing mists cold and gray like curling pattern within a marble agate, agate, cat's-eye explodes from impetus of thumbnail popped against its backside. The splash of sound of color as prizes career from the charmed circle. Over here boy do this pair of dying shoes. Cecil couldn't even afford the dime shine, but let himself forget one moment. Listened to the jaunty song, met the one dancing eye.

—Ah go on, mistah. Shine make you pretty. She'll like you pretty.

Cecil remembering shook his head no. Told the shoeshine boy with movements of his hands inside the torn lining of his trousers that nobody was home to pay for anything. Cecil smiled whistling the boy's ditty. Shine. Was not so long ago had my own hustle on the street corners. Could pop a rag. Carry a bag. Cecil Otis Braithwaite little boy rimed to himself. Right down there with the rest I did my best. Fever in the funkhouse looking for a five. Rattle them bones. Seven come eleven Nigger goes to heaven. Pay the boss, poor hoss lost. On his knees. Marbles, bones, the grimy coins changed hands. Down and dirty in the street. You ever seen a dog do it. Doggy water is what you make when you shake it. Till it grows up. On your knees makes holes in your pants. Patches. What pirates wear over eyes. Captain Kidd. Popeye the sailor man, did it to a garbage can. One-eyed kid smoking a butt. I would give a million for your song, for your smile, for your lost eye. Do the shoe, do it and you can have everything.

–Nothing, you ain't got nothing.

–Just enough to get my hair cut, and I must get it cut.

–You's all right, my man. For you I'm gonna do it free. A lick and spit just cause you gonna be something someday and maybe you remember Shine that one-eyed boy on the corner.

There were scabs on the back of the shaved head bobbing below Cecil's eyes. He can do it though, can't he. First time in how long these shoes feel wax and a rag. Perhaps the boy heard, could see me all those years ago making my hustle. Scarred bowling ball works so hard. And then the eye and the bad teeth. Long lashes an awning when he lifts his head, when he smiles up at me and one moist, dark eyeball disappears into the top of his head.

Walk a little taller Cecil your shoes are shined. Bottom to top you shall be a better man. The boy's song faded into the dull hum of the streets. Cars passing, doors slamming, the broken talk that had to climb dark stairwells or walk the tepid air between hot brick walls. Going home for a haircut.

–Dat's the man. That's the magistrate.

–He ain't no magistrate, ain't no man. He ain't nothing.

–A big faker.

–Yazzuh, a big, black humbug thinks his sweet ass got wheels.

–Give the boy his quarter. That's his due.

–Mister magistrate of nothing.

–Humbug magistraitassed uppity nigger.

The voice had been hidden on cat belly beneath the cool rot of some decaying stoop. The voice could not be heard above the drone of flies or maggots inching their way along the particolored spills of rusty garbage cans. It was more quiet and humble than the short puffs of air Clara fanned up under her dress to cool the damp kiss of her loose thighs. It might have been a roach snoring or the scurrying rodent feet that panicked at the dark, pulsing cat shape prostrate beneath the cool rot of some decaying stoop. Cecil didn't believe the light tread hardly heavier than air, but almost before he could disbelieve, the needle point bore into his flesh and then too late to do anything about, wings and thread legs perched on his arm drinking, drawing up the blood from his heart.

—Pay the boy, magistrate.

Cecil counted the coins in his hand. They were holy beads he fingered, trying to squeeze some metaphysical life from their dull, round shapes. The introit, the Angelus. He told them one by one, entranced, anxious, dreading the sum, the full circle.

—How much do you want.

—We want you, magistrate.

One-eyed boy moved to the edge of the group that was gathering. The rag was still, both eyes glazed and unseeing.

—I've done nothing wrong.

So then this cat they call the magistrate starts to fidgeting. Like he knew all the sudden niggers weren't there for no play. No, man. He commence to counting and looking around, down at his feets, cross at the boy, side to side at all them hot nigger faces.

—I have done nothing. What do you want.

—Boy said he did them kicks of yours then you walked away without paying him nothing.

Then the mag says slowly looking from face to face:

—There is some misunderstanding. The boy did the shoes because he wanted to, because he felt like it not because I

34

promised anything in return. Ask him if you don't believe me.

—Shine, is he lying. If you lied to us, Shine, I'm going to have a piece of your ass myself. And as if busting one head was just as good as busting any other them niggers starts to grunting and pawing the ground and Big Tony shakes a fist big as the shoeshine boy's head about one inch from that blind darky:

—I mess up that other eye for you if you lying.

But the shoeshine boy ain't for no shit and out comes his razor:

—Nigger you lay that hand on me and you gonna draw back a nub. Now Big Tony ain't no fool and when he sees the boy one eye all lit up and that blade standing tall and clean he cools his heels and grunts but don't move one inch closer.

—Put up your sword into the sheath. The mag stood there like he really was some kind of special body and strangely enough the boy did put back his knife in his pocket and all the rest didn't barely move just froze in they tracks like waiting for another word.

Ich hab es euch gesagt, dass ichs sei, suchet ihr denn mich, so lasset diese gehen.

—Let him go. If it's written that blood must flow, I'm sure it was meant to be mine.

—Well did the mag cheat you or not.

The shoeshine boy spoke and when he did it was like words from a rock. Both eyes was dead cause he didn't blink just stared straight ahead with the dark one and the light.

—He ain't no friend of mine and if his shoes was done it was cause I expected a quarter.

Everybody had crowded round now like they do when theys the tiniest excuse just to get close to each other and make heat. Off the stoops, outa the shade, from corners, boxes, kitchens, windows facing the street all them gathered round magistrate Cecil and the one-eyed boy.

–Don't worry friend it's me they want. They'll always want me. Go your own way. It is done; I am delivered.

–The man is crazy. Like all I got to do is give free shines. He ain't no friend of mine. Out here to get what I can. Give nothing away, asks for nothing. Shine for a nickel, shine for a dime, shine for a quarter if you got the time.

–Let him go.

Wine smell was high on the air, especially you could smell it on the cat's breath who sidles through the people till he got right next to the magistrate and splat with the palm of his hand loosened some jawbone and made Cecil spit red.

–Who you telling what to do, nigger. You is in trouble if you don't know it.

Magistrate Cecil shook his head, swiped his hand cross his lips and commenced:

–I have only said what had to be said. If I've done wrong or said something wrong tell me what it was.

So there was the mag soft talking and trying to move down the street with all them niggers crowded round him. Close as white on rice. He was like a stick being carried away by the gutter or a leaf in the wind. Kinda in a daze it seemed to me I don't mind saying I felt sorry for the cat. Afterall he come to grief just trying to do some of the things most of us would do if we could get together the right shit at the right time. Who wouldn't like to walk through this jungle with his nose high like he couldn't smell the scum and even if the filth could rise up to his nose his nose held so proud and holy it couldn't be touched or hurt. Always that piece of suit and some kind of rag tie you could tell Cecil thought something of hisself and wanted to make something of hisself. The way he talked when he would talk. A book caught in his throat or a spoon shoved up his ass he dropped each word like an egg that hurt him to lose and like if he didn't get it out just right it might crack and be yolk all over the front of his shirt. He did keep a clean shirt. Holey and frayed but Esther did keep the nigger clean. Everybody knows what a fool that woman is. Thinks she got a good thing, she thinks when his day comes he's gonna be a big man and all her slaving and saving pussy just for him will pay off with loads of gravy and goodies ever after. Too bad that child don't know magistrate Cecil will drop her yellow ass quick as he gets the chance. Same old story every time. Some good woman hauls a cat up, kills herself doing his dirt, then one day he says goodbye, goodluck, I got a younger, sprier, prettier hen. But getting back to what I was saying, off they went with Cecil in the middle leaving that shoeshine boy singing on the corner.

–Never seen a fool like that. Like I'm out here for my health. Free. Did that nigger say I said free shine. In the boy's fist a quarter from the hand of Big Tony from the pants pocket of Cecil from the vest pocket of Henry Gitenstein, thirty-fifth in his class at the university law school.

2

"Ole Rileeh walk'd in wahder"
—Leadbelly Song

HARBOR BELLS TOLLING, DING DONG PIPING
whistleshriek ou whee, ou whoo, *Bee Ohh*.

Heaving subaqueous heaves and shudders the land like a table rolled from beneath a magician's horizontal assistant in a demonstration of levitation left the ship by inches till miraculously Cecil was afloat.

Seaborne.

Stubbornly groaning and wheezing that lingering menagerie of cranes, lifts, drydocks, tackles, and slurring chains was put to sleep. Only blinking lights now that studded the shore in formless profusion, lights identifying the prehistoric reptilian shapes only if the viewer abstracted his iconography from some mythic overlay that isolated horizontals, verticals, pairs, and triplets and with the astronomer's irrepressible metonomy yclept this Orion, that the Dipper, those eyes there the dinosaur who spewed my trunk into the hold. Cecil had watched the loading, the lowering, awkward beasts and thick men who tended them. Handle with care, with fragility. Made in Japan. Maid in Germany. Union maid.

Flags and flowers and the scurrying crowds chased by whistle toots up and down the gangplank. Kissing in the corridor. A door slamming farther down the passage. Summer sailing and all's well bluesea beckons a band plays. We are going to war, we are conquering heroes returning. Beneath our feet the Trojans in chains hold their breath. Some of the slaves are sick with anxiety yet hold the curdled fear behind their teeth, choking themselves because they fear a greater torment than that of their own suffocating insides.

Embraces become more public, more passionate. I expect those red quivering fingers there to slide from the waist that cleaves to them down down past the pinch to the blooming fullness there to pat and fondle and at last raise the skirt push down the panties and a cheek in each fist down to the marrow squeeze, down to the deck drop and never even be missed. I am seeing machines that line the dock, boxes, crates, vehicles drawn to shining attention. I see acrobats on the swinging ropes. I see a tall lady with an upraised ice-cream cone toasting the emperor. I see in what must be the west how fast the sun drops. A moment ago one side of the city was brazen, each window molten with the heat of its own brilliance. Buildings that were ingots of blazing bronze, gold, and copper. This against mauve of flocculent clouds trimmed in gold. Now purple bellies higher more somber, gray of sky meeting gray towers of city. Monuments in a humble churchyard vying for attention, crowded, vain, a ragged silhouette of withering stone.

Winking now, they offer constellations, significance to be deciphered. I see rivers, flotsam and jetsam. I hear myself hissing, a candle drowned.

Dear father, father in whose black home I see so many stars blinking, tell me, father, do all journeys commence with such questioning, such tumult and confusion.

Some sign. A comet cutting deeply through the blackness, red meteors glowing in its tail. Here we are drawing the sea closed behind us, white, ghost churning, invisible ripples outward, then nothing. Sea zippered shut in our wake. A sign would do, anything you could do for us since afterall we are launched, we cannot bargain, hold out for an overwhelming demonstration. Assure us not of a special destination, but that we are destined, intimate no portion, just that there has been an apportionment.

Why did you do it.

–Sometimes you are very much like him, Cecil. Below the Alhambra they sat talking in a café, Cecil and Webb remembering rooms in other cities, other worlds.

–You mean your son.

–Yes, like him.

Around the fountain a room grew. Circular the pool, circular the benches, circles blunted to octagons climbing one within the other to a vaulted ceiling. Fountain splash trifling like someone peeing in the sea.

–And is that why I'm here?

Windows in the white walls. Pictures like stained glass depicting pageants, saints. Windows Netherlandish framed in thick gilt and gold. The dozing, gray museum guards.

–I can't answer yes or no to that. I think at times you're here purely by accident. When I say you are like him I don't mean in any obvious way. The first time I saw you I was aware of no similarities. At most he was approximately your age when I saw him last.

–And your son, he was black.

–Color yes, but even that was quite different from yours. Darker in fact. Anyone could see he had Negro blood. But his build, most physical details differed from yours.

Above them in the Moorish castle a room and a fountain. Fountain was a pride of roaring lions. Tribute from some oriental monarch to the conquering black kings. Onyx lions whose throats spewed twenty foot geysers which cascaded to white turbulence in the center of a deep pool. Continuous gut deep reverberations, lions growling hunger, anger in a marble sepulcher which echoed their yearning. Stalactites hung, ice transformed to marble dripping from the arched ceiling. Where the black kings laved their bodies, underground, surrounded by magnificence, symbols of obedience, of power, the coolness and rectitude of geometry, symmetry celebrating the peace within themselves.

—And the picture made you speak.

—The "Adoration." No more than it made you answer. Not until I knew you for a while did I begin to sense important resemblances, points of contact.

—To your black son.

—Yes, my black son. But in the museum, in front of the picture, the first time I saw you, what drew me to that particular place was the Bosch painting you were standing beside. Then I saw you and . . .

—You said there was a better version in Madrid.

—Something silly like that, and the rest followed. The rest was easy after such a foolish intrusion.

—I was nothing, no one, nowhere. It was impossible to intrude on *me*.

—So you said yes to my proposal. Let me take you to the Prado "Adoration." Three thousand miles away. And here we are.

—No strings attached.

—And still none. You have your return ticket. I've given you sufficient money to make travel or other things feasible. But here we are, still together. No strings attached.

—Cecil sees the world. Cecil white man's burden.

—That's how I mean. Like him.

—You didn't know him, you've admitted that many times. You say you only saw him once. Or that you've seen him only in your imagination. You contradict yourself continually.

—I don't know you, Cecil. But like him you've decided to wrap yourself in old sorrows. To be a kind of walking, talking *lest we forget*.

—But it's just that quality that makes me needed, makes me loved. Earns me expense paid vacations to Europe. I run into the nicest people, people just begging to be reminded.

—The word bitter keeps wanting to be said, but I'm sure

44

saying it about you or him would only be another way of turning my back.

Cecil stared; it was the look he had given the Magi.

—And if I go now, Cecil, will you promise me that you'll follow on the day I asked?

—Why then. Why not a day before or after. And if we split up now, we might as well keep going our own ways. Break clean just as we met.

—I tried, Cecil, honestly I tried to tell you why. But the reason, the story, is so incomplete in my mind. It would mean much to me if you would just do as I ask.

—One week from today. The end of Semana Santa in Málaga.

—It's very important to me that you come.

—I'll go back to Madrid. I'll wait six days then I'll go to Málaga. But why Málaga . . .

—Why you Cecil. Why me. Why this table three thousand miles from where we started.

—Then you'll be leaving tonight.

—Always leaving it seems. Running somewhere.

—Or away from somewhere.

—You are like him.

—You've given a lot to me.

—Please. Just come. Nothing has been given, much is lost.

Cecil's eyes had been dazzled by the Prado's black king. The long neck of the Magus, the richness of his garments and the elegant page by his side. Not a man who had just happened, who had yesterday learned of bright colors, precious metals, the dignity in the folds of a robe. The Nativity was alive in a way the other one hadn't been. A final statement of the theme, repose, assurance, simplicity.

To say yes. Yes yes yes yes yea saying again yes yes again to say it yes yes yes yea yea saying I am yes. . . .

I will go yes as you ask. Of course I will go. Image of

45

image in water. How one is upside down will not stand still is deep yet floats on the surface is really neither down nor up nor does it end or extend that still image of itself above water.

I was on a ship. The land moved away. When it rains or when I stand beneath a fountain I am underwater as the image is neither under the water nor on the water but shadow of that which is itself still shadow.

On that promontory My Friend is the seemingly impregnable citadel of the Black Kings. Defied all of España till on a White Horse Iago Matamoros cleansed the dark plague from dis Land.

At the foot of the hill, barely visible from the ramparts of the Alhambra a café called La Gloria, consisting of twenty-nine chairs and a kiosk, reinvigorates those who are about to ascend and those who have descended from the fortress. Cecil alone.

Es muy bonito aquí, no señor.

I read: potpourri of architecture. Additions made throughout its existence. Each incorporating prevalent style of period of construction. Succeeding kings each attempted to make personal impression on structure. Can be viewed either as combination of many individual parts or complex unity reflecting not so much definite plan as a continuity that has the shape of history rather than logic. Restorations, additions, buildings razed, left partially constructed one century, completed the next. A tension between new and old if not completely satisfying aesthetically, at least vigorous, realistic, and honest.

So in the shadow of the walls I dream and drink gin. Webb is gone; my promise is gone. I review the history of the Moors in Spain, the Reconquista, the pogroms. They say the gypsy quarter at night is exciting, authentic. Brown bodies, brown wine, brown music. Not brown of business

46

shoes but that black tinged, red tinged blood-brown of gypsy skin.

Of all punishments the poet said the greatest is to be blind and in Granada. These words inscribed on the castle's walls. A high thick wall that secludes the intricate, almost effeminate gardens, where bearded black kings were wont to stroll with maidens carefully selected from the cowering red-roofed houses below. Maidens chosen as scrupulously as chargers—color, gait, fineness of teeth and mane being not the least of qualities ascertained. Maidens who would feel the subtle silks of the East for the first time on their skins. The scent of orange blossoms, lemon blossoms, frankincense, and myrrh languid through the delicate trees and shrubbery, scents which alternately lifted then pasted to their soft skin the diaphanous, caressing fabrics that had been arranged on their bodies by smiling eunuchs. Maidens whose eyes widened afraid of some pagan sacrifice when led past the roaring onyx lions till down through cool subterranean passages they were put at partial ease by steaming baths and sherberts tingling through their warm insides. So strange that black hands, gnarled bark-backed warrior's hands could be so soft and smooth, could intoxicate the white tenderness where silk parted silently.

Why did you do it.

She tossed me an artificial rose. I had a table close to the platform on which they danced. El Cinco Flamenco. Two hundred pesetas to enter, one fifty a drink. Cab driver who took me to the gypsy quarter screamed he had been cheated when I refused his first tabulation.

I closed my eyes and heard a jackhammer ripping the sidewalks apart. Their gypsy heels clacking, clacking louder and louder, ball and chain striking feeble walls which collapsed in a dust wheeze of weariness and gratitude. *O lay O lay. Baila Hombre!*

47

I kissed the Rose.

Gave it later to a saucer eyed urchin who wandered into the bedroom just as my pants and drawers finished wobbling up my legs to embrace my bare ass. I gave the rose and an *adios* to pass on to her mother, who had disappeared as soon as her ablutions at the bedside basin were over.

Esther, In my fashion.

First but not the last it began my tour, my quest. Don Cecil, undertaker of perilous journey, seeker of knowledge. Knight of the rose made flesh, the carnation.

The narrow ship plies backward and forward relentlessly. Someone, even if only part of myself, to talk to.

Notes on THE PRADO—April 19

Luis Tristan 1600
> Sad upgazing saints—Santa Monica, Saint Llorosa

Hericlatos crying

Juan de Juanes—pyramids—in background leering mustachioed faces. Martyrdom of St. Esteban cycle—sun draws apex of pyramid toward it.

Cena de San Benito—austere, dark, frugal cubicle of hermit. Brown shadows. Two studies, old men's faces—drinkers, cups in hand.

Zurbarán—little color, muted shades, chiaroscuro, browns, grays; simple like monks' habits he paints—bold relief effects—objects in isolation because of monochrome planes of color, blackness of background—relief almost—one red cup startling because it comes in midst of gray, brown, black darkness. Unnerving—fresh blood in an empty room.

Ribera—much in common—only red appears in large amounts—the only "color."

16th cen. anonymous—Judith con la Cabeza de Holofernes —Esther's body—nipples, breasts, torso exact—widely spaced breasts, pronounced cleft to navel, flatness of abdomen to pubic mound.

St. Sebastian's martyrdom? Santa Catalina. A city, an automobile, almost Simon—St. Simon?

Mural painters, 12th cen.—Angels with eyes on hands, feet, wings. Saints with curiously tilted heads, as if just hanged. Impossible contortions—angles of limbs, hands, feet inhumanly flexible—supple like the fins of fish—repeating the undulations of some fluid, invisible medium.

An old woman who has a potato breast, wrinkled, brown plantlike tendril droops from tip. Old man prostrate in a tentlike hut—attended by two demons, snakes, toads. Old woman with burning hair—dogs—cats— monster in saucer hat, veil, trunk protrudes beneath.

Pieter Brueghel—"Triumph of Death"—1520?–1569— dogs eating dead children—army of skeletons at gates of city. Man hung from crotch of tree—man chased by black dogs, he guards his genitals.

Head of goose—phallic, pallid, fondled by a cherub same color. Gooseneck like a snake crawling into bottom corner of frame—sheet music—a violin—Virgins

My Pietà—one I drew from wall of church—D. Crespi— Jesu Cristo Difunto

Teniers—monkeys

Clots of tourists meander by. I think it is not a desire to confront the paintings but the language of the guide they follow. The sounds he makes are reminders of home and simple concerns, the common accents of native speech which each can share though the members of the group are strangers in a foreign country, trespassers who at best conspire among themselves beneath brittle canopies of sound maneuvering through the corridors and galleries. Is there a guide for me, will one come along who knows how I must withhold my assent until I translate any language into that black subterranean one which is my own. I am unprotected. I am tempted by French, Italian, German, Spanish, any and all of these bursts of sound seem appropriate as they float by. Not a linguist, nor a citizen of the world, just equally a stranger in all the tongues parading past.

And the pictures. Can I move among them without the aid of some impossible interpreter.

It is different, alone this time. I am calmer but more desperate. With Webb as guide I seemed to have some purpose. We were in Europe because something awaited us. It seemed almost as if we had a timetable and appointments to keep. But now that I know he is waiting for me, I have no sense of purpose, no feeling of urgency or direction.

I think at times I am on the edge of a great awakening or at least a realization. Something to do with understanding Webb. What do we share. Where have we been. Always backward, always to the past. I associate museums with him, certain rooms in libraries. When he is on the verge of talking about himself, I feel he has begun with a tacit *Once upon a time*. His self-revelations come like chapters of a nineteenth-century novel, shaped, interlocking with that pervasive sense that life owes some unpayable debt to literature. I think of Proust in his corklined room, but a Proust who has lost the thread of his own experience and reads rather than remembers. Perhaps because I have so little past I know of, I am jealous, or at least hypersensitive to what Webb has accumulated. Perhaps I am intimidated by his continent of archives and documents.

This is my last trip, however, to the museum. When I see

Webb again I am afraid I will be impatient with his stories. I dread enough the mystery of my own past without entangling those longings and memories with another man's dream of himself. There is nothing I want to return to. That is why I am here, a stranger. I need no more temptations, no gods to serve.

The "Garden of Delights." I am a horseman in the enchanted circle. Others ride beasts magically corresponding to their species of damnation. Leopards, lions, camels, oxen, bears, hogs, deer, unnameable eclectic mounts, haunches of bloodhound, head, chest, and forelegs of an eagle, pelicans on a goat's narrow back, mounts and mounted leisurely around a charmed circle in whose center a still pool with naked women standing thigh deep in dark liquid. Black and white women their slim bodies exposed in provocative poses to the circling riders. Surface of pool broken by hands and arms of couples who copulate submerged like frogs. But the riders are barely aware of the pool and women. Some are burdened with monstrous, outsize fish, others are aroused by the closeness of nude male flesh, the sensuality of the beasts they ride or some narcissistic game they can play with touch, smell, taste, feel, and sound of themselves. Birds hop, perch, ride, fly, hover, drink, eat, sing, and screech within the scene. It could be the procession toward the ark in its profusion, its universality, yet that image modified perversely so the pageant of life projects its greediness and absurdity rather than an orderly, calm progress toward salvation. Men and beasts in an arbitrary hierarchy, even an arbitrary stability of form amuse themselves as best they can within the closed circle of the sensual dream.

I hear one of the maidens singing. The black one who sits on the edge of the pool, the one with the graceful peacock on her head. She elegantly holds a piece of fruit aloft, either beckoning or considering its plausibility before devouring it. She says come play with me in these warm dark

51

waters. Hurry, hurry she teases. She asks if I am a man or simply another of those riders round and round again.

Cecil didn't want to sit. Standing in the circle of green tables and chairs that surrounded a striped refreshment kiosk he gazed slowly upward and outward relieved by the brilliant afternoon sun and serene stretches of blue sky. As usual Bosch had disturbed him. Even the ridiculous Spanish title bestowed on him—El Bosco—with its associations of chocolate milk, cookies, and talking cows in Cecil's mind did nothing to dispel the foglike gloom that seemed to seep from within the canvases. An adolescent reaction, or even more, the primitive revulsion of a child. Some threat seemed contained in those apparently chaotic, incomprehensible masses of movement and color Bosch had created. An undulating ridge in the background or a color rhythm would suddenly assert itself, begin to dominate a composition. And this order, this moment of pure insight when the kaleidoscope gathered itself into a pattern, would make the nightmare world of demons and evil in which the vision existed surge forward full-blown into life. Cecil could hear Bosch. The screams of the dying, the damned, those already whirling in the vitus dance of hell. Today the moment of insight had been almost unbearable. Even now in the open air, in the sunlight, slight tremors passed through his body still echoing the tumult that had spilled from the "Garden of Delights."

Finishing nearly half his glass in a clumsy gulp, Cecil blotted the beer foam from his lips. He believed that only a madman could truly understand Bosch, and that only a man periodically insane could have painted all he had painted. Bosch had studied the crippled and deformed. He knew a madman's eyes, the blank, expressionless stare of the living dead. He knew how they sat and stood, what they dreamed. Bosch awakening from his madness to paint, fascinated like Dostoevsky by all manifestations in other men of the raging darkness he feared in himself. Perhaps searching for something to prevent another plunge, or perhaps just feeding the hidden demon while it sleeps.

—Heya, buddy . . . why don't you sit down here.

What struck Cecil was the way the burly man seemed to surround the table at which he sprawled alone. The man's red elbows leaned on the table's damp surface. He was hunched forward so that his Hemingway beard covered the backs of his hands. If the round table had been twice as large, Cecil would still have felt he crowded the man.

—Cross there . . . to the museum?

—Yes.

—Something, ain't it. Yeah. I go there myself. Lots in that place. Say, could you spare a man a fag. Cecil pushed the opened, silver case toward the man. Already he had become familiar with the strange bright object, its incongruous richness was natural in his fingers. One of the hands emerged from beneath the beard, and thick, blunt fingers dug out one of the offered cigarettes.

—Nice case. If I was the kind of guy that kept things, that's something I'd get to keep, a nice cigarette case. One with a lighter built in. Yours got a lighter . . . no . . . but you know what I mean anyway. After you give a broad a fag you snap the case shut, solid like a Cadillac door, then press some button or something and up jumps the fire. All this time you're still leaning in her face smelling her hair and she's leaning in yours and she's impressed like hell. Everything in a fancy silver box. She knows you're the kind of guy gets things done. Efficient. Right down to business type and silver . . . but I'm not the sort to keep things.

53

–If you don't mind me saying, before I called you over, looked like something was bugging you. None of my business, I know, but it was noticeable as hell to me and I wasn't doing anything so I figured I'd call you over, figured you wouldn't mind me mentioning what I saw.

–I don't mind. I wasn't even aware of what I was doing.

–Not what you were doing. You just looked damn strange, like you were being chased.

–That's close.

–Just telling you what I saw.

–You did see a man running. Something inside the museum. It had the power to drive me out here to the street.

–Made you almost choke on your beer.

–I was thirsty.

–That's what I said. And you can believe what I say though I don't think much of talk. It's my eyes that work for me, and half the time I'm not listening to other people . . . just watching. Tells me more than words. When I talk, it's about what I've seen, not other talk. World's too full of people talking about other people's talk.

–You probably have a point.

–No, no. The point is you don't know anything about me. And you don't know if what I say works or if I work it. You've only heard me talk. Watch me. See what I do. That's the point.

–I've seen how you can use your eyes.

–A good beginning. I'm Albert, friend. The man rolled the cigarette between his fingers. The red, freckled forearms and thin biceps exposed by the rolled shirt sleeves were unattractively disproportionate to the man's brawny trunk. Cecil thought of a beetle's dark hulk darting along on stick limbs. Cecil lit a match, but then hesitated an instant, intimidated by the combustible looking mass of reddish beard. Smiling the man leaned toward him.

Albert drew deeply on his cigarette, exhaling a light

cloud of smoke. His brown eyes were moist and bright as
his smile broadened; he pointed a thick finger at them.

—Ha. Eyes, man . . . eyes. They'll tell you what there is
to know. I warned you, I'm a watcher. Did you think you
might burn poor Albert up? The bearded face moved back.
Smoke curled up again, this time from wide nostrils. The
features lost their animation. Cecil saw a middle-aged man,
a man with a rather scruffy ginger beard, a hairline already
receding far back upon his square brow. The man's skin
was coarse and weathered, its permanent ruddiness as close
to tan as alcohol and sun could change nordic white. Cecil
imagined that the beard hid square jowls that had begun to
sag and go flabby. A peasant face. Brueghel. Lots of beer,
sausages. A man on the downhill side of prime—limbs beginning to shrink, the limacine middle expanding, flesh
disintegrating into the beard.

The eyes lit again. Catlike Albert rubbed his broad back
against the metal slats of his chair.

—You didn't say what was chasing you.

Cecil realized for the first time the size of the eyes. They
were tiny; their brilliance not their size dominated the face.
Lines sharp and precise marked their corners. A swatch of
dark brow above and purplish flesh beneath made the eyes
seem deeply inset.

—Believe it or not I was frightened by a painting.

—Painting, huh. Why not, why the hell not. If you're the
kind of guy that gets frightened, why not a painting.

—You've never been frightened.

—Well shit, man . . . never by a painting.

—By anything.

—Not a painting. That's what we were talking about . . .
paintings, right. Hell, of course I ain't a fool. I mean there's
some things in this world a man moves for. I mean a tank
or eagle shit if he sees it coming. Stuff like that any fool
moves for. But that's not being scared, it's not being a fool.

–But what about something that can't knock you down
or dirty your clothes. Something that . . .

–Something what?

–I was trying to get you to answer a question I don't
even know how to ask. If you have or haven't been afraid,
doesn't matter. I'm going to have another drink. Can I get
you one?

A man and a boy sweated inside the striped kiosk. Neither saw him till Cecil placed two glasses on the counter.
After a moment the man raised up from the block of ice he
was chipping into a small sink, nodded at his customer, and
looked disgustedly at the daydreaming boy. Shouting, he
slammed the pick once more into the ice then kicked and
cuffed the boy toward the counter. The boy cringed as each
of his clumsy movements in the tight enclosure brought another outburst from the man and a violent thrust of the
pick. Cecil wanted to catch the boy's eyes. To smile at him
or wiggle his tongue at the man bent over the sink, anything
that would draw some part of the boy out of the cramped
box. But the boy hid his eyes beneath heavy, black lashes
concentrating on the awkward movements of his own
brown hands as they opened and poured two bottles of beer
into two glasses.

When he turned again toward the table, Cecil saw the
bearded man was gone. He felt relieved, conscious of his
entire body responding to the sky and sun as it had after
being released from the vault of the museum. Cecil looked
down at the two cold glasses in his hands. The second was a
joke, a dream, joke glass he would drink himself or pour
onto the pavement. Then he heard the already familiar
voice:

–Put 'em down, man. Albert ain't gone nowhere. And
hey, get another. Albert was in the middle of the broad
Paseo del Prado. Bearded Albert one arm around a long-

legged woman in a short, tight skirt continued to shout and curse as he returned through snarled traffic.

—Bringing a friend, my friend. Bringing Estrella to meet you.

Estrella's long legs were bare. As he approached with a third drink Cecil watched her cross them, leaving most of their slim length uncovered.

—Estrella . . . this is my friend.

—*Buenos días* . . .

—C'mon, none of those bows and that *buenos días* shit. Estrella ain't *señora* to nobody. This old girl is what you call *puta, puta,* man, and that means whore, tart, bawd, streetwalker, pussy, fucky-fucky in any language. Right 'Strella. The woman smiled at both men; she wrapped long fingers around her glass nodding to Cecil as she raised it to her lips.

—Strella, Strella baby. You got drawers on today. Albert's thin arm slid under the table. Cecil felt the sudden bump of ankles against his as the woman started in her seat. Albert's visible hand was quick and caught the flashing purse she aimed at his head. His eyes sparkled, coughing spasms of laughter shook his thick body.

—Strella you got as much down there as I got on my chin.

Hissing something between clenched teeth the woman jerked her arm free. Beer lapped onto the table as she pushed her chair away and swung her legs out into the open. A perfunctory tug at the black skirt was the only way she qualified the nakedness exposed to Cecil. Tossing her head in Albert's direction she spit loudly into the gravel.

—Whore acts like she got something down there I don't know about. Well I can tell you, my friend, she's done better tricks for me with those lips than spitting. One thing I can say for her. She knows her business. What's she sitting around here with it hanging out if she don't want somebody to pay attention to it. She must think she's in godblessamerica where they can wave it around like Old Glory and not get it touched.

Cecil lit the cigarette he had given to the woman. Her thin lips were painted mauve.

—Whatta tell you. Her eyes ain't left that silver case since you pulled it out. If I was the type guy who kept things, I'd have one. Yours don't even have a lighter and look at her . . . like a moth after a flame. Kill herself to get to it. Go on. Grab a little pussy yourself if you like what you see. I'll be damned if she does more than smile and let you dig in.

The woman was a sphinx as Al talked. Wine and brandy succeeded beer and somewhere in the progress from bar to bar, woman disappeared altogether, an unnecessary mouth, an evolutionary dead end in the efficient movement from sober to not sober of Cecil Braithwaite and Al, his thirsty appendage.

Foot tapping to guitar music, mouth full of chewed peanuts, leaning on his elbows Cecil nodded, his features screwed up a moment as if swallowing a belch, but then he was smiling, a giddy, silly smile.

We were children running on the beach. Old grace. She was French, German, Spanish, Russian, sun tanned and dark haired a body I had known so well night long as she lay breathing cocooned in sleep beside me but now we trotted at the sea's edge teasing the foam flicked rushes setting a hard pace, splat of our feet lost in surf's crashing.

Wind beat our faces, sucking out breath. Legs still good but this hungry wind empties the lungs. Down we go sprawled on the sand. Rolling into the sea it takes us gasping, sputtering with a sudden swell. Hands and knees high we scramble out. Down again, bronze crosses on the white sand. Words taste salt as tongue moves across ocean wet lips. I am mystified by the language we are using. Wind cools the off side as we sit up, blinking back the intense sunlight. When we run and splash and die a bit on these sands, I am as alive as I have ever been. I have been alive only this once, pushed dripping wet from the sea. But we are singing an old, old song, song older and bigger than born or unborn. Are we the first or the last two.

Up a rock El Moro mounts, gleaming sea birth. Atop and pissing a parabolic stream caught by the wind. I promise myself to spurt thusly into seven seas from seven continents. At rock's base breakers crash, rumbling over the coral reef, gaining momentum and fury as they sprint the last blue gap and extinguish themselves brutally on the black rocks. Can't help laughing as spray reaches my face, as my stream ended and breakers in heat rushed to thud and die beneath my feet. Laughter, loud, rolling over the muffled explosions below, I was as high as I had ever been. El Moro's bare feet find niches on the rock's slippery surface. I grab at her hand, pulling her up so we could laugh together. Peals of it mocking the ocean's dull thunder and its thousand deaths, trembling together till spray and wind managed to chill us in the brilliant afternoon.

You leave in order to lose to find.

Es muy bonito aquí, no señor. El Moro grins. His awe-giving jack boots reflect the bar's brass rail, grind the sea shells and peanut shells and sawdust.

—*Sí, sí, amigo. Cerveza.* And you lisp glib tongued the Castilian lisp blackly bellowing San Miguel with proper intonation and from the bottle after wiping rusty lip with heel of hand gulp one half of contents to wash down the shot of gut eating brandy.

—*Felipe Segundo. Uno más, señor.* An arm went around the powerful shoulders and a voice, a stranger's voice whispering something about slowing down about how one mortal sin in Spain is to be drunk and show it. Cecil conqueroo turned to meet the challenge. The stranger's eyes dropped to a glass the waiter had deposited, twin to the one clacked down in front of Cecil. If the man saw the belligerent flash of El Moro's hawk eyes, or the sudden combat tautness of neck and hand, he ignored them. Sweet booze looseness eased the conqueroo. It was Albert's red arm upon his shoulders. Albert who was speaking.

Albert was an expatriate from southern California, whose sun he had often followed across the border into Mexico on liquor raids. Marijuana and *señoritas* for a five buck, crowded car hop on weekends. Thick necked, square shoulders, a big man whose imposing exterior had begun to soften. Hair on hand backs; Dutch descent. Tales of South America with its Latin propensity for hot blood, political revolutions, dark-eyed *chiquitas,* massacres. The dead stretched in rows across an empty field. He had a picture of it; a smiling general all teeth and brass two minutes before he was machine-gunned. Album of violence. Uniforms. Bravado. High black leather boots, Sam Browne belts, a peasant grinning with a pitchfork. Albert, tow-headed, very young posing with heroes who pledged land reform, but brought tyranny. Always sun. Dust rising behind a vintage tank. Rubble. Smiles. Albert armed, posing with the deposed. Jailed. Front tooth out grin. A pumpkin. A hairy-handed Dutchman, rectangular, wooden dikes inside his belly and chest. Spain. Last resting place of the Hemingway breed. Oh, the good old days. Blood. Spirit of the revolution! Gone. Whores commercial, timid bulls, a brash, mustachioed little man stamped on deflated currency. The sun. Yesterminute. Albert disgusted. His Swedish wife home again, home again with her admiral father who never liked him in the first place. Just left her one day. Couldn't take it any longer. We had two kids, blond, plump as *Blutwurst,* he presented another photo. Always the little things. Fine when we were alone. When we could come and go as we pleased. Always together—nights in tents, under stars, railroad stations, a barn. Scandinavia produces damn good women; they learn early up there what it's all about.

But the brats, they made it different. Impossible. Little things like hours, silly obligations, give in, give in. It's them now. It's their turn. Live for them. So I just left. Five years now. She's still young; I was the first. Twenty years difference between us. Probably your age. Since then I haven't been doing much. Just drifting. Munich to Madrid. Sometimes like a ping-pong ball, sometimes like a feather. I've been trying to write a book. It's my last hope. But it won't come. Just little spurts. Anecdotes. Not even stories really. Pieces. Like me, bits and pieces. Jew hater, lover of a Jew. Munich to Madrid. Like an old train stuck on one unfashionable milk run; hoping at best to be taken off active duty altogether. Retired to a pasture. To rust and be climbed on by children. Hulking shell of a toy, all movable parts removed for salvage. Not even the dignity of a hole. Tears in my beer, huh? Just a passing fancy really. Just seeing you, hearing you talk about the things I know so well, seeing you looped on this gut rotting brandy. Echoes sometimes. I'm an anachronism, friend. There's a certain security in this. Last of the race. A dinosaur. Determined not to change, not to compromise, to go down brilliantly futile and obsolete. Then seeing you, my kind perpetuated, takes away the vestige of pride left in being unique. I'm sorry. Just one of those whore evenings. Why doesn't one of those greasy bastards sing? When you want quiet, can't keep them off the top of the barrels, stomping, clapping, yelping like castrated coyotes. Get up there and sing you cunt mouthed Castilians. The good old days. Yesterever. Now you only have to yell fuck Franco to clear a bar. Scared. All the proud little greasers scared. Sing somebody. Sing or I'm going to get on that barrel myself and curse your ancestors.

Nobody hears. Nobody cares. Just a row of backs and

asses staring out at you. Sorry, it's just . . . sometimes it's like this. I mean not even somebody to fight. You know you're the first colored guy I've ever really talked with. To be frank, don't think much of Negroes. About in the same class as Jews, except a little better because they don't have as much money to spend. I guess it's more true to say I've never known any. Don't really care one way or the other. A few general things against them though; couldn't depend on them in the war. Bad outfits. Not worth a damn as fighters at all. That was an accepted truth at the front lines. But after what we've been talking about, maybe I can understand some of the reasons why. Hell, I guess it was tough. Especially then. Catching hell from both ends. And your generation or rather in particular you, if you're any indication, you're saner than any of these effeminate scatterbrains I see making the grand tour. Sick, pasty faced, pimply bastards. Not one ounce of blood in a dozen of them. Afraid, that's what they are. No background, no roots. Saucy and fresh, ready to throw mud, smear disdain. Tear everything down. Every man that's ever done something is a square, an incompetent. They discredit every real personality that's ever existed, the ones who have built this world that the punks piddle around in. They try to bring the great men down to their level because they know they can never rise up. Afraid. Smart, rude mouthed little punks vomiting undigested wisdom, covering everything with their filth. I can smell it, feel it. That's what's killing me. Everything tight, no spice, no freedom, no place to go. I feel sorry for you. It's gonna be worse for you. What was your time, when was your age? At best a counterfeit nostalgia for one you never had. Maybe mine, maybe one that never did exist. Alone. Not strung out between two worlds like me. No improbable Colossus of Rhodes, no, you can't even plant your feet in a small doorway. Nothing. I feel for you.

62

Just a question of going back for me, burying the young man, the only thing I can or ever will be, but you can't bury him till you get to be something else. A question of standing up. Looking back and seeing what happened. That's my story. What I have to write. This mess, this world about to lose its guts, I don't care about and don't care to understand.

Albert's face. Far away, coming from eons ago, heroic, immaculate, armored in his own strength. Mountain tall, his will implacable as man leveling club at his waist. A child rushing heedless, headlong, believing wholly in a brash trumpet clarioned in the crystal air. Believing. In love with the simplicity which rolls all the world into a ball, carrying him with it out of the trenches, and across no man's land to pile up singing on intricately wound clumps of barbed wire. Selfless, immersed, or squat and unconcerned as barrel on which someone has begun to dance. In the café. Albert rehashing forever. Cheap brandy resting on odors of the rancid *bocadillos* hung in bulk on the wall or bite-sized in open dishes lining the damp bar. Lyric almost, Albert's self-conscious keening. A surprising delicacy, eloquent as each snowflake that dies to make the ponderous drifts.

Albert loving. Releasing from behind the stolid dikes a sheaf of photos he kept with him always, stuffed inside his offensively bold, open-throated plaid shirt.

Ashes, ashes, we all fall down.

Wail of flamenco from the jukebox someone had turned up. Albert's voice *sotto, sotto* as if music were a dark curtain hurrying to enclose the drama. Cecil swayed, either inwardly or with his body rocking. Not the sickening lurch of the stricken ship, but the dance of bare treetops in the wind. But a proper metaphor was nautical, was that natural correspondence of boat to medium, the exchange of self-centered gravity for the water's embrace, its rhythm and power, its eternity. To be a captive. To be the drunken boat, to release as Cecil knew he had released all illusion of control.

Albert explained that the background song was the chant of a prisoner, a condemned man, who had killed his unfaithful mistress and her lover, but from his cell shouted that he would do it all again, take his revenge even in the face of God and of greater punishments than his captors' could possibly threaten. Al could anticipate the singer's moods, his laments, the warbling screams, whines, animal modulations of voice which re-created scenes from his story. Flamenco passion, echo of the conquering east still brooding over the land. Cecil was uneasy. Incongruity of Al seemingly moved by the ghost music of the exiled *moriscos*. Or perhaps just the sadness of the song, the lonely voice, the utter isolation of the soul trapped in a cage with only a memory of betrayal to dream.

But El Moro had come to town to laugh to drink and fuck and forget. At home an uppity nigger, thinks he's smart, all dressed up, Magistrate Cecil parading down the street like he owns it. But here, El Moro. Whatever else they think about the dark foreigner, they remember in their blood that he once had the upper hand, that they paid him the conqueroo's tribute, that he was a teacher.

Song is finished a second time through. Cecil wants to speak, to tell Al . . . or is it just a desire for a monologue of equal time.

–It's funny how you carry that black crap inside you. Like the time I wandered around in Granada needing a haircut. Walked past the damn barber's ten times. Looking in, trying to figure what he'd say, if it was O.K. for me to go in, plop down in one of his white chairs ignoring the fact that I was black and had kinky hair. All that crap churning inside me—afraid, embarrassed, mad at myself for being these, for being different, mad at him, at every white man for making me uncomfortable and mostly just shame that I couldn't bring myself to walk in and sit down. Well El Moro finally said fuck it and went in. It was like nothing, I waited my turn, got in the chair and he sheared me like any other sheep. A little conversation. As much as I could manage with my eighty-two words of Spanish. American. First time in Spain. Thank you. No more. Good. Paid and gone. Painless. Just me, carrying all that bile inside myself. Cecil Braithwaite Transporter of Plague Incorporated. First three thousand seagoing miles free. Guaranteed safe delivery.

El Moro cannot see across the waters, yet from the other side they see him. Voice of his dead son; Esther's voice less than ghost but living, beckoning. Her dowry.

Why did you do it.

Al's eyes are glazed, two antique, polished coins laid atop the closed lids. The bodega's interior had gone to mist and black impenetrable smoke. A bier is launched and the mourners on the shore's edge are dark silhouettes, miniature skyline of a fog-shrouded city. Is it proper for the dead to speak when spoken to. Gentle rhythm of the narrow ship. Cecil cradled serenely by beer, brandy, and wine. Being here is being nowhere and everywhere. The passage is everything. Destination as unreal as that quiet city already lost in the gloom.

It is afterall part of me. Trader Al would have made his fortune camped in some calm inlet; he would have hacked back the jungle with his heavy Dutch hands and built a limbo village of cages beside his spartan hut. Warriors would appear with other warriors in chains, with children and females huddled together in the shadows of the men. Al would Dutchly wheel and deal. Sampling now and then a Negress to reassure himself of the quality of his product. The Great Western Civilizing and Trading Society with branches everywhere. I was the burden Albert chose to carry. Mongo Al, supervising the middle passage from darkness to light. But I am tired of travel, weary of dancing once a day to whip music, nine-tailed cat songs. I grow old, I grow old. And must I remember older sorrows, nakedness, hunger. Did they come bearing gifts. Was it wrong to squat catatonic and die staring at the sea.

There is a storm. I am angry beyond anger. I hear the splash of bodies heaved overboard to lighten the ship. Some go unnecessarily because a frightened sailor miscounted and disconnected one black wrist from another. Waves, thunder, and wind, but the doomed in one last futile triumph are heard above the tumult.

I am tossed, tumbled, enraged. But storm settles and for better or worse some survive. Albert burping beside me survives and I buy him another drink.

The men move on. Festival time. Relentless flogging ends for a thirsty week and the streets of the old quarter are full.

El Moro dances:

Rosa. It had to be a Rosa. What other name goes with olive skin, high cheekbones, flashing eyes and white teeth. The whole bit. My twelve-year-old gypsy of the incredibly happy smile and jet, never-ending hair. Dancing together flamenco style and the crowd loved it. We sent some kids to buy more wine and passed it all around spudie-udie. Fifty pesetas slipped into Rosa's hand, the first touch. Always. Gypsies shouting—*olay, olay Rosa. Baila hombre!* El Moro *baila.* And I must have fled to find this street.

El Moro battles:

—Should I hit the son of a bitch.

—Forget it, man, there's too many of the enemy.

—C'mon we can take 'em. You ain't chickenin' out on me, are you, Al.

—I'm right here, man, but there ain't no win. You hit him and every little bastard in the cave is on our asses. You know they carry scimitars in their pockets. And we bleed, my friend, we bleed.

66

Albert, the nuns have cloistered your bowels. Up there on the hill, in jars, are your intestines and balls swimming in alcohol. A preservative you know. But Sister Angela Maria Duessa. Her guts blew away. Dried up, and one day a little dusty cloud descended from under the folds of her many black skirts. Spoof. They were gone. She told me it was a kind of warm leaving. A pleasant, very intimate closeness then separation, warm, almost like a fart.

–Next thing I knew the fascist sons of bitches threw El Moro in a cell with a bunch of gypsies. Smelled like a zoo. All those greasy little bastards, piss and barf all over the floor. Musta been the drunk tank. Smelled like hell. Stale wino pee smell. And I ain't in there a minute before one of them starts vomiting. Splattered on my boots. I pushed him away and he fell. Straight down. He musta been real drunk cause splat he buckled right in the middle of that steaming shit he just finished bringing up. Then three of 'em was on my back. I was whippin' hell out of any I could grab, but somebody got to my face and scratched me good. Son of a bitch tried to tear out my eye. Look. I'm gonna get a tetanus shot tomorrow. Just like animals, little filthy animals— gruntin', sittin' around in their own shit.

–How'd you . . .

–So this weasel beneath one of those plastic toreador hats he smiled a yellow toothed smile and began to beat me. Goddamn Civil Guards. Heavy, flat sounding blows across the cheeks then a hollow thudding noise as leather coated stick slapped against my groin. I was so ossified didn't feel a goddamn thing. Just worried a little about how close he was coming to my gonads. Wino laugh. Pain no part of me. Remembering it would all be over in a few minutes, like reading in a newspaper about atrocities being committed in another country. Laugh saved my balls. Everybody started laughing, all them in those cartoon hats laughing away. Then they kicked my ass out of jail.

El Moro loves:

Keep off the grass said a boot to the drunk who woke with pain and found sun in the sky overhead, fountains of the square dry, nowhere to be found those gaudy lights or music or the swirling dancers so many whose hands and backs and cheeks he had touched or where was it I kissed her, hot tongue probing deep in my throat and a bouquet of hair, all black, elastic yielding, it was hot there and wet, popping back the nylon panties snapped against my wrist. I think I remember a doorway where from my charger I leapt down, her with one arm lowering from his flanks and then I began to forget and how much petticoat, won't those ruffles ever end. I began to forget the frills, the scalloped edges, all wet they were her lips and inside me something not me moved hot like an animal in my mouth and if I am very still the blood will stop, nothing no nothing will I feel nor will these hands push and pull, popping elastic too tight here anyway for a whole hand, *señorita,* squirmita, I could love you on these stones, no one will enter this darkness, but first my armor, let me remove these obstacles, obstacles, obstacles so hot and dry like the skin of a dead snake I found once, forgotten where it lay, where it lay forgotten kick, kick me again—*Olay*—I am falling. I give up, please forgive, please don't kick, forget, forgive, I promise never again. O father, father forgive me, forget me, let me forget that I have skinned, that I have sinned, forget me Father, no more please for I am dying, do you hear me, dying, you bastard, pop pop pop soon it will break and room for five fingers, can you take five fingers I remember once there was a girl we all went to her in a car and when my turn she smiled over a clump of weeds and she was wet and purple and something had been eating her flesh and left raw running wounds, she winked and beckoned hurry, hurry from behind the weeds her mounds of fat and sunken like a patient on a table slowly opening, closing, the bush winked a bird flew out and died on my head, streaking my cheeks with something, with blood, sweat, or perhaps its white, dainty excrement, and I ran from the room but that was then and now I would have shoved my foot up the hole and shut the door if she screamed like she did as she straddled the gleaming machine strung out in pain, having her uterus scraped but better a quick pain than one looking at you everyday, a dusky, kinky haired one from her womb so let me hold your hand as you writhe and please be careful Doctor for in this moment I am bound to love, bound to love as you catch the drippings in a pan, pan getting filled God where did it all come from one black bastard made all this mess hold my hand and don't cry, it is better than seeing it grow, than hating it more and more each day, oh how they wail and shit and scream and the pain growing everyday please believe what I say Esther that this is best that I love that I will never let go your hand though it burns and squeezes and drains feeling from mine bone against bone you grind it and wriggle on the shining machine wide open will it never stop coming, never stop never let me sleep I must get up and turn it off don't be afraid I'll be right back, Esther, then we can sleep I will tiptoe and turn on the light only a moment, just for a moment on then it will stop we will be able to sleep and dream and dream and dream.

And if he hits me there I will be a choir boy. My voice will not drain away into gonads and hairy cheeks. I will always respond to the master's flaccid wrist. Higher. Higher. It is so beautiful here, is it not. Ruins of a Moorish castle on the left. Best one in Granada. Right above you, madam. Yes . . . black. Black kings. I don't recall exactly when, but long ago. Arabs and niggers. Long ago. But that was before the pill. Perfectly safe now. No pain. No more calls from a pay phone telling me to put in my diaphragm. I'll be home soon, dear. Do you understand. I came to find to lose. The fear. Fear of what's on the other side of the door.

There is to be a celebration the last night. Oh sure I'll be there. Meet you at the hotel. Bells on. Cap and bells. Celebration in the gypsy camp. An ox is to be slaughtered. *Cristo Negro's* hands dyed crimson in the sacrifice. The streets will be crowded again. I must hurry . . . find my place . . . find Rosa, the singing . . .

The plain which is the threshold of the city curdles with the stench of unburied corpses, dead men rotting in the sun, bodies with soft insides already pulpy and boiling, heat blackened dead wandering through the maze of shanties and hovels, through impermanent, weather ridden heaps undignified by stone or monuments, the human soup laced with rag and cardboard and splintered boards that seeps from the city in an ever widening pool. The poor of Madrid, compressed between hot, dry clay, and the heavy sun into bronzed bricks that will build pyramids to honor the Emperor. It is one more canvas to observe, a *pièce de résistance* after chasing El Grecos in the low hills surrounding Madrid. Toledo with its Alamo, Thermopylae don't give up the ship Alcázar and the villa of the painter who perhaps could not see straight. I wanted to remember names —the paintings, the chapels which housed them. But it is the narrow streets which I recall, afterimages of heat white when I blink my eyes. The favella is a giant rancid sponge, sopping wet that clears the blackboard. I smell and I taste and the postcards I had dreamed are in shambles.

Suddenly as if to say you cannot forget everything, I noticed that in the distance the horizon seemed lower and an El Greco sky was forming.

Rain, it would rain in the city, on this sick plain. But not rain of Verlaine's ballade, not a human rain that completes

70

a mood, but just water, feverish and exhausted water that had dropped then spiraled invisible back to clouds only to drop again and be sucked up again from puddle and sea bed to drop again. Water that already had tasted the dead and would return this knowledge to the land. Rare, pummeling rain that drenched Cecil as he sat listless in the tourist bus lumbering down from the hills into the city.

Rain or sweat tepid inside his clothes. It was hard to tell, to understand. Speaking out would make a difference, clarify things. But to whom. Would the dead comprehend his obscure language. Would a few downtrodden songs chanted in chorus relieve them of silence, and of distance. But if the vehicle paused Cecil knew he would keep his seat. His destination was no more this teeming shantytown than it was the teeming hard city. Estrella, Webb, lying, extravagant Albert who had caught Cecil in childish dares. Estrella's scent still strong on his body. Webb. The Webb. Follow the leader.

The night air made Cecil shiver involuntarily. He could see no stars above the fluorescent blue shimmer cast up to rooftop level by the neon lighting. His hands were in his pockets. He didn't really watch where he walked, letting himself instead be jostled along by the light pressure of the crowd which was taking the long way home through San Jerónimo's narrow, twisting streets. Like the fish and mushrooms frying on open air grills, Spanish spit and crackled around him. He expected to see a fight beginning after each explosive exchange, but only saw bright teeth and eyes, smiling men and women with hair groomed and shoes shining no matter what they wore between these extremes. The women were colorful schools of fish, self-contained, outwardly indifferent, discussing their curiosity among themselves in whispers as they glided past. Clusters of men attached themselves quietly, a natural condition of the seascape, making no obtrusive signs of possession or even

71

of the right to approach. Lone females would appear in force later, though they often traveled in pairs. Cecil noticed a few already drinking alone in cafés or surrounded by laughing groups of bare-armed laborers in the cramped interiors of bodegas.

Estrella would soon put in her appearance with the rest. Would anything be different this last night in Madrid. Albert waited for him, not far away Albert waited, certain like the woman was certain that he must come. Each day Cecil had promised himself he would not go to Estrella, but at some point during the night he would find himself in a taxi rushing to her. Once in a drunken dream he had mounted her, ripped the sore of her from within his bowels, heaved up his rage and need in one humiliating assault after another upon her flesh. He had awakened sweating and impotent in her bed to the reality of her laughter and her fingers kneading the dough of his sex.

She lived with her mother in one of the government housing projects near the Plaza Monumental. The women kept their small apartment very clean. Bedroom, kitchenette-dining room, and a sitting room. The last was Estrella's pride. It contained a thick pile rug, an overstuffed sofa and chair, a glass topped coffee table, a television set, and most of the time her nearly blind, senile mother. One night Cecil had sat with the old woman close to three hours waiting for Estrella to return. The mother had been silent and expressionless the entire time. An occasional blink was all Cecil had noticed until the television station had ended its transmission and the room was plunged into darkness. Then except for a slow belch which had relieved the stillness, Cecil could have been in a room with a corpse.

When Estrella finally arrived that night she had company. The sailor was drunk. He swayed in the doorway, disconcerted by the light Estrella had switched on and the two people it revealed sitting wide-awake in the dark. Cecil

72

couldn't make out what the man muttered to him, but understood the leer at the old woman. Estrella's mother did something to the thousand lines of her face, screwing them into the grimace of taut exertion she must have believed still approximated a smile. It was her greeting to all her daughter's men, as constant and forgetful as the vertical lips of ˙ Estrella's nakedness. It was what had greeted Cecil the first night and what had been repeated just as uncomprehending each night since.

Estrella had kicked off her heels and padded across the rug to turn off the television. As soon as her daughter and the sailor left the room, the old woman curled herself into a corner of the couch and lowered her head onto a shapeless pillow covered with yellowed silk. Her snores were not loud enough to smother the sounds from the other room while Cecil waited.

This last night he wouldn't go. If the old fear returned, he would bury it in some other whore.

Cecil thought it strange that only one woman had sung to him, to him alone as part of their love-making.

Cecil walked to the end of Ventura de la Vega. After a few more steps, he could see the bright sweep of the Puerta del Sol. In its center twin fountains sent up high, swaying jets. The wind that had carried dark clouds over the hills whipped ragged skirts of spray around the silver columns. On the long awnings of sidewalk coffee bars and in huge letters on the thick, blunt buildings that faced the plaza the names of the beers they drank, the clothes they wore, and the banks that owned their mortgages smiled down on the people.

Cecil made his way from island to island of security till he finally arrived on the other side of the impossibly wide plaza. He wondered how long it took a cop to learn to control the countless streams of pedestrian and motor traffic which converged on this arena. He was dazzled by the sudden onslaught of motion and brilliance. It was entirely different from the intimate activity of San Jerónimo, from the ambiance that had allowed him to linger over his meal, the wine, his thoughts. Here cars careened at a pace that could kill. And they came from all directions imparting their urgency with violent trumpeting and shrieks. Wide, bare spaces hostile and forbidden to those on foot isolated the cramped plots of safety. Once Cecil had wanted to dance between the fountains, El Moro naked except for a cop's white sun helmet and Sam Browne belt. The memory of that first day made him shiver. He thought he felt the chill prickle of white spray blown onto the back of his neck. As if pursued by a dark shape materializing out of the night, he entered a bar.

The bar was too bright; its harsh, yellow light had weight and substance. Cecil could feel it like a swarm of insects settling on his skin.

—*Felipe Segundo, por favor.*

—*No hay, señor.*

—*Cuarenta y tres . . . grande . . . doble.* Not quite certain which word to use, Cecil placed his hands together then moved them slowly apart. The old fish story. Bartender smiled, nodded, in a moment delivered a tall water glass three-quarters full of brandy across the counter.

Where Cecil stood the counter was glass. Behind the glass on shelves were displayed a variety of confections. Farther along beyond the glass case the bar was stone-topped, with a flat wooden edge facing outward. Saucers containing the snacks that seemed to be essential for Spaniards when they drank were ranged on the marblelike slab. Cecil could distinguish slices of squid, varieties of sausage, mussels, boiled eggs, anchovies, cheese, pickles, tripe, crayfish, peanuts and olives. The contents of the other dishes were unguessable, but seemed to be devoured at the same rate as the ones Cecil could recognize. Men were shoulder to shoulder the length of the bar. At the rear of the long, narrow room mirrors extended the bar and the line of men forever. On the sawdust strewn floor heaps of crayfish shells and legs had collected under the footrail and banked against the spittoons. Like breakers, clots of sound from the far end of the room gathered force then hurled themselves toward the street. Saucers and glasses slammed on stone, the cash register's incessant ring, the excited jabbering of the men, washed over Cecil. Through the open doorway Cecil was surprised to see sidewalk tables belonging to the bar. When he had entered, he hadn't noticed the green metal tables or the well dressed people around them. He bolted his drink, then cautiously picked his way through the tables and the milling crowd away from the Puerta del Sol.

Albert had said he would be there most nights, that he would explain, justify. It was a short walk to Calle de Jardines and Calle de Jardines was a short street. In the middle of the block was a shoddier than usual bodega Al had named. The bartender proprietor pointed out to Cecil the name of his brother, Manuela, which was listed among many others on a disintegrating bullfight poster. A gray, cracked mirror two feet long and a foot wide was the only other embellishment of the wall behind the bar. A bead curtain separated the private and public halves of the owner's dwelling. Against the wall facing the bar three empty wine barrels served as tables and chairs. The predominant tone of everything was dull, dirty brown. Plaster dust rained continually from the exposed beams of the low ceiling, and with gestures, grimaces and a few words of English, Carlos, the owner, complained bitterly about his lungs. He made it clear that he didn't get enough sun. That the tall *pensiones* across the street were too close and he was dying in their shadow. But he could not leave because the men always came to drink, to sing, to eat his rotten *bocadillos* and dance on the tops of the empty barrels.

The rain finally came. Somehow the night grew even darker. Calle de Jardines seemed to be in the storm's center. Before Carlos shut the crooked door Cecil listened to the flurry of panic, the rapid footfalls, banging shutters, women's shouts at the heavy drumming of the first big drops. No matter how long or ominous the threat, it was always like that when rain descended at night on the city.

Albert lumbered through the yielding curtain, his ham hands fumbling with his fly.

—I ain't the only one doing some pissing. Sounds like the whole heavenly host squatting over this town. He smiled round the room and crossed himself. Hearing his rumbling voice several Spaniards looked up from their wine, saw the pious gesture, and repeated it.

—Figured you'd be here sooner or later. I see you beat the rain.

Ignoring the voice Cecil reached for a narrow tumbler of brandy Carlos had poured. Quickly it was inside him and racing for his belly. New and raw the cheap spirit was a ragged current sending heat back up into his throat. The smell and taste lingered. He could always tell when a sick night was coming. Early in the process of obliteration one drink would be like this; his senses would recoil, the bile rise warningly in his throat. Some nights he knew his body would refuse the outrage.

—Prithee, Cecil, why so pale and wan?

—I don't feel playful. Let's come to the point quickly. What you said . . .

—Trimmings, Cecil. Trimmings are all. Just being my usual protean self. Saint, sinner, dunghill of flesh, suave courtier. Whichever you like. A man for all seasons. Even for rainy nights in Madrid. Tell Uncle Albert whatsamatter. Rain, rain go away. Cecil wants to play.

—I said I'm not in the mood.

—What mood then. If not versatile, I'm nothing.

–Just don't be the fool. Let me drink another drink and try to relax. There's not much time. No time. I leave for the south early tomorrow. You relax, be quiet for a moment, then please say what you have to say. Cecil recalled Bosch, the demon at the saint's ear. What had been said. Webb's face appeared, ghostlike, at once vulnerable and distant. The promise. The artificial rose the dancer had thrown Cecil in a clip joint later that night.

Rain splashed the cobblestones and swirled in gutters. Already from ancient, tile roof spouts rivulets cascaded.

The men moved to the back of the bar. Albert buddha-like draped the lotus of his buttock on one of the wide barrels. Between his feet a nearly full bottle of Felipe Segundo rested. Cecil stood, his back almost against the lisping curtain. Leaks in Carlos' front door let in stabs of cold air and oily snakes crawling under the door began to twist through the cracks of the stone floor.

–What did you mean when you told me to relax. Dammit, man, I think in the whole universe there is no mass which has more inertia per pound than I do. Like here I am sitting on this barrel. If there was wine inside this wood, it wouldn't be any more relaxed than I am.

–O.K. so maybe you're relaxed. But what you're doing, what you said had just the opposite effect on my nerves. After your story, those crazy warnings that first night, you knew my curiosity would make me come here. Now it's late, now I want to hear everything. Or at least the rest, why you wanted me to see you again.

–I wanted you to talk to Albert some more. To hear some more of his stories, get to know him, maybe even tempt you to forgive him. There is much to forgive, and shame, betrayal. I wanted you to bid Albert a fond farewell; I wanted you to listen again, hear me say why you can't see Webb. For your sake and his. I knew the cigarette case, saw his initials, but I knew it was his before I saw them. I

77

guessed he gave it to you, I told you I knew him once, and you told me the rest. You told me lots I'm sure you don't remember. Not hard to figure even if you had said nothing. He wants you to meet him tomorrow in Málaga, last day of Semana Santa. Jesus Christ, man . . . I repeat: get your ass away from here as fast as you can. Albert kids you not. Stop the mothering thing.

They were pig eyes, scared pig eyes at last recognizing the butcher. The body would be stuffed in the vat it now so cockily rode.

–No sense, no sense to it all. This place . . . Webb . . . me here . . . the rain . . . you and that ridiculous beard. Matted with every conceivable filth. Do you ever wash it.

–No, my friend, not me. You didn't come here to insult poor Albert. Besides I don't always hide from the rain. You're exaggerating. I stride naked into it and angel piss makes me clean. The beard too. That and all the other hairs with which I'm festooned. But you don't offend me. I see a bigger picture. It's not me you resent or the occasional flea who might reside upon my carcass in a dry season. I see deep, dark forces at work. The worm, the mole, things that crawl, creep, and burrow underground. They're blind when they strike out in the light. You do not offend me. And do not apologize. I see your hasty, and I am not being spiteful if I say nasty, words hurrying back like so many boomerangs to rankle in your bosom. Do not apologize. I see the big picture.

–What . . . just what do you see.

Albert snatched up the bottle of brandy, a red slab of hand wiped across his lips.

–You know what I think—this purple-bellied bottle is half the secret. Cheap booze and donkeys. Every country has a secret—you know, something special that holds it together and makes it what it is, makes Spain different from Germany and Germany different from England, etcetera, etcetera. Well, without cheap booze and donkeys the bottom would fall out here.

—What do you want, Albert.

—Look at them. The spics. Big, brown flies, flies heavy like when the weather turns cold. So damn easy to swat them then, I give up the sport. Swollen with the offal of what they've been. Nothing worse than those buzzing bastards when they slow down and begin to die. They don't swoop down any more, just fly over something and collapse. Hara-kiri for that one last sniff, that last chance to rub their legs in shit, to buzz-buzz and drag their wings across your donut. Look at them leaning on the bar. Like they all just shot their load seventy-five times in a row. Making love to Carlos' booze. Queen Carlos. I used to think that he worked for them. But my eyes told me no. My eyes watched them begging for what he has, my eyes saw how they loved him, how these flies think he is the grandest, cutest, stinkiest dungheap in the world.

—Grow yourself a mustache. Get out in the sun and bronze that shit-brown skin of yours. Make it black if you can. Then get sandals, a beret, and clothes like those you see them wearing. Go to the outskirts of town and find one of those donkey trains, the kind that don't have people with them. When you see one like that, let it pass till the last little old donkey's ass is about a yard away. Then just fall in behind. Donkey trains go round and round the earth forever. Somewhere, somebody's building a big hole. Peopleless donkeys will take you right to it. You know those sacks they carry. They're full of dirt, nothing else, just bags of dirt from that big hole. When the hole gets deep enough and wide enough this country's going to slide right through it. Then the rest of the goddamn world. But this country first cause they own the donkeys. Like water going down a drain. One loud fizzle, a burp and nothing left. Just the donkeys circling a void loaded down with sacks of nothing.

79

But you go and see for yourself. The hole ought to be big enough by now to let you and everything you want to take with you get through. Of course I can't say if it's small enough to keep out all the things you don't want. Been a while since I've seen it. I'd go again, but I get tired looking up a donkey's asshole.

Cecil poured more brandy in his glass. It was innocuous now, sending no messages to his brain. Outside rain blew in sheets through Calle de Jardines. From roofs water drained downward to find the smooth depressions it had been licking for years into the pavement. A baby's sharp cry, distinct and angry, floated from a high window, fading till it blended with the rush of wind and water.

—I don't know what I expected, but I'm certain I was wrong to come here tonight.

—It's damn wet outdoors. There's a lot to be said for being dry . . . and high.

—Just tell me . . . no, tell me before you drink or pour the bottle. Was there a son? Who is Webb looking for?

—Who? There was once upon a time a young man. Webb fathered a bastard on his black mistress, Anna. Webb has been waiting years for the boy to come to him. He still believes somebody would travel three thousand miles to say God knows what to a perfect stranger. When I met Webb, he was searching for his son and paid me to help him. It didn't take me too long to figure out the situation. I had fallen into just enough madness and money to keep old Albert going in his declining years.

—And Webb. You feed his delusions. You attached yourself to him just like you did to me that night.

—We search. When I saw you with the case, I was scared to death. I thought to myself what the hell's going to happen to poor Al if Webb has really found what he's been looking for. It was tough with Webb in America. He

80

wouldn't take me along, but I knew he'd be back. But I was damn sure he'd be alone.

—And I am to be this son to Webb.

—You are whatever you want to be. He's waiting. The streets are full, but he will find you if you go.

The pig eyes widened.

—Cut me in whatever you do, please. But for Albert's sake, for your own too, just forget about Webb. What'll happen if you go to Málaga tomorrow. What could happen. He needs his dream of a son, not a son. And could you act out the part he'd want you to play. Could you stand up under all that guilt and remorse he'd want to lay on your shoulders. Could you forgive him every day a hundred times a day for the woman he betrayed, for his blindness and unfeeling hands. Whose life would you be living. Come on. You're a sensible guy. Stop this before it goes any farther. You can't change what he is now so give him back his ghost. It's the only decent thing to do. Let me lie to him. Let us go on playing the game. Go home, Cecil. He isn't as rich as he seems. We just barely make it. Leave us in peace.

One by one the children die. It is this fact that makes the sun unpleasant on my back. I can hear the sea, the wind and the gulls. The pages of a book rippling. Sand thick in the air covering everything.

When the sand beetle begins his climb, I will kill it. He came from nowhere, armored, prehistoric, and after sunning himself, is ready to crawl over the yellow mound of sand. Beetles crack like nuts. Nougat centers surprisingly white. I raise my fist. . . .

Someone said no Charles no panic almost in the voice.

But there I was on the edge dreaming of the long plunge, of the scream that would leave me breathless.

–Doctor. Dr. Webb. I have a lady, Doctor. Would you please come in. The room is so small and the company unpromising I know you wonder what you're sitting next to— cancer, flu, hemorrhoids, morning sickness. Then starched white the saving angel comes: Next.

You cross the threshold.

–It's going to spoil everything. Don't the fools understand what's at stake? Everything we've worked so hard for. Sometimes I lose faith, begin to think that we've been wrong, that the crackers know what they're talking about. Blind rage, ignorance, and bloodlust. Killing and looting now of all times.

–But how do you expect people to understand?

–I don't expect everyone to understand. Not yet anyway. We're just beginning to make progress. The men who count are finally reacting, money and power slowly pledging themselves to our ideal.

–And you want . . .

–Patience. That and nothing more. After all these years, and the time and effort so many of us have put in. Delicacy is the key. You can't imagine how important it will be to find an appropriate language for the most fundamental questions.

The train passes through a broad, green plain. Nothing taller than nodding grass as far as the eye can see.

The little staircase was so flimsy and treacherous that Robinson did not often go down into the crypt where the mummies were.

First the shadow then the white hand touches the page. He turns down an edge. There is sand in the ridge where the pages meet. From his hand yellow-gray grains cascade. Whisper then hiss as a mound is formed on the spread-eagled book.

Bardamu Bar Damn you Bard an Mew

Meanwhile Old Ma Henrouille kept things going on in the depths below. She toiled like a nigger over these mummies.

It scuttled black and shining within my reach.

—Like everyone else, I suppose, I just want to feel that I'm free. I wouldn't know what to do if somehow I were turned loose.

—But you are, you know. *Loose,* as you call it. Now, this instant, what keeps you from getting off that stool and walking out of here.

—Doctor, you realize . . . of course you must realize . . .

Someone running in the wet sand. Feet sound like flippers. And children laughing. Perhaps a game of tag. The sea lapping up and swirling round their ankles. The sun.

Stop chewing your pencil, Charles. Charles, did you hear me? I said stop chewing it . . . you mustn't . . .

When Charles received her letter, he thought of the word *disdain*. Anna had taught him to spell the word: *disdain* not *destain* as he had written it twice in the short story. He had been annoyed at first, wanted something more from Anna than the schoolmarmish quibble, had to exert tremendous control over himself not to shout or strike out when he saw her precise handwriting and the little bracket she had inserted in his manuscript. Until that moment he had never felt so distant from her. The penciled correction was a rebuke pure and simple. Her chiseled word *disdain* over the chaos of his own barely legible scrawl could never be removed. At the periphery of his resentment had been something that for a long time afterward had managed to remain remote. But now as he slid his finger into Anna's letter, he remembered the whisper of fear, his gradual recognition that something profoundly disturbing had elicited his disproportionate response, that the word *disdain* leaping up at him from his page had intimated all that would subsequently take place between Anna and himself.

Slowly he cut through the blue airletter. To Charles Webb watching his hand clumsily part the dotted folds the whole progress of his life in time seemed no longer or shorter than this passage of his finger through the paper. In fact the ragged edges seemed to him a perfect metaphor for the wake he had left in time. But his trail had closed, a knife cutting water. So it had seemed with Anna; with all things. He knew the letter he spread on his desk would affirm this truth. Anna would be a different woman altogether, mother, wife, tourist, after twenty-five years making the much delayed and longed for grand tour. Would she ask him for travel tips, for hotels, restaurants, a list of good people in each capital to visit. Perhaps in her careful handwriting grown more ample, more decorative, more *feminine* in twenty-five years, she would tactfully offer to secrete the grave of the past, landscape over it a green, cheery memorial park by introducing her husband to Charles and the progeny she knows he'll just adore. He was sure at least the letter would announce her imminent arrival. Nothing short of such a drastic removal could have caused her to write after twenty-five years of silence. Perhaps her husband was dead. Perhaps she herself was dying prematurely and had chosen some bit of beach, some set of strangers to die among. The consumptive ebbing away in the brilliant sunshine. One final, corrupt tug at life. The street boy who would crawl from her death bed and strip the jewels from her corpse. All these morbid fantasies took their turns in Charles' mind. What Anna had been to him had climbed back into its limbo after the word *disdain* had flickered then faded from his mind. His random thoughts, the little plots he could fabricate were an attempt to establish a mood, a tone that would give import to the reading of the letter. As it lay on his desk, it was curiously insignificant. A vacuum surrounded it, nullifying the possibility of any response, making it impossible to treat the flimsy piece of paper and its words as a reality. Anna and what she chose to set down on paper belonged to a dead time. The man to whom these words were addressed and to whom they might have meaning had ceased to exist.

With resigned respect and solemnity as if a priest were crossing the arms of a corpse Charles folded the blank flaps of the airletter back upon its body. So long to reach him. So many dead addresses canceled. But finally in his hands. After glancing down once more at the two strange names on it, Anna's and his, Charles tucked the letter into his back pocket.

Charles often suspected that it was an affectation on his part to keep the tiny *salle de bonne* at the top of Hotel St. André des Arts. Years had passed since he had written anything that would justify the keeping of a studio. The tomb-like room with its steeply sloping ceiling, the tortuous staircase that led to it, the sudden bare walls and boards of the uppermost level contrasted theatrically with the worn but still pampered elegance of the four floors beneath. But the room had been cheap and elevated enough to temper some of the street sounds so Charles had found it suitable for his purposes. Though it no longer served any vital function, Charles felt that its former services deserved some lasting reward, some monument, so instead of relinquishing his lease he indulged his sentimentality. At one stage the room had been for assignations, but much sooner than he was willing to admit to himself, the labor demanded by five flights of stairs outweighed the titillation he received from what was vaguely erotic in the room's shape and seclusion.

Of course, as he perpetually reminded himself, the room would be just the thing for any friend passing through the city. But as he crossed into Rue St. André des Arts moving toward his studio he knew it would be empty, and that it had languished tenantless for longer than he cared to remember.

M. Jacques, the porter, greeted him. At one time Webb's association with the short, bald man had been almost conspiratorial. When women had shuttled in and out or the American alone would spend days locked up in his loft, M. Jacques' professional curiosity had been aroused, and he had enjoyed fabricating a secret life for his guest, a history documented and enlivened by significant nods, winks, gestures, the intonation and emphasis in a *çà va* or *bonne nuit* in the lobby. M. Jacques compiled volumes listening to the tread of Webb and each new companion upon the stairs. Shy, certain or uncertain, leaning upon each other, or a leader and follower, rhythmic in step together or the stumbling wine dance and finally in the quiet darkness of the hotel, from high in the vault of the stairwell the closing of the last door. M. Jacques was now nothing more than polite. Like the bells in small Paris shops he registered Webb's entrance with an automatic echo of cheerfulness. The porter's mind never left his thick ledger and its ornate, close-columned calculations.

Through the room's one window a dull light like a coat of yellow dust broached the obscurity of its interior. Webb stood in the doorway, aware of his heart and lungs, of the machine's dependence on its finite, vulnerable elements. His cot, his writing table, his lamp, his chair. Charles pulled the string that dangled from beneath the hood of the gooseneck lamp. The lamp tilted forward as it always did, but just before its equilibrium was lost Charles laid the palm of his hand against its fluted base. The thick metal was cold. A ridge of dust came off on Charles' hand. Acrid smell of dust burning rose as the bulb heated under its tiny reflector. Its circumscribed glow only accentuated the room's shadows. Charles engaged in the familiar struggle with the window, finally wrenched free the inside metal retainer and using both hands pushed out the double panels.

Traffic sounds of nearby boulevards reached him rather than the morning activity below. Like its residents some Paris streets awaken early in the morning, but others who find themselves busy most of the night and sometimes till dawn arise leisurely, refuse to acknowledge another day's beginning, resent the sunlight's intrusion or the premature striking of a footfall through their corridors. On Rue St. André des Arts the arrival of shopkeepers in their long blue dusters, the rattle of the three-wheeled milk wagons, the postman's boots were interlopers in the somnolent morning atmosphere, activities that had commenced only in the dream of the street, which continued its slumber.

The writing desk had one small drawer. Turning from the window Charles opened the drawer and drew three notebooks from inside. Two black, one red, they contrasted boldly atop the desk where he laid them side by side. Quietly as if to conceal the movements from himself Charles took the few steps that were enough to examine each corner of the room's interior. He stopped beside the cot, stood glancing down at the counterpane, attempting to distinguish its faded pattern from the mottled shadow patches imposed by weak light coming in at the window. Abruptly he dropped onto the bed, raising a puff of dust that writhed through the narrow band of sunlight floating beside his dark figure. Charles closed his eyes and leaned back against the wall submissive to the confused flow of his thoughts, not yet admitting the inevitability of certain images, events and personalities, pretending that the plunge into his memory would not be structured by his particular fear and desires, but some arbitrary, soothing logic of the unconscious itself.

Charles Webb, his head now resting on a thin pillow rooted from beneath the dusty counterpane, his body bowed to curve of unresisting springs and sagging mattress, became a thing inert, as bereft of volition as the instruments he had disturbed by entering once more his cave of making. The window, the lamp, his chair, his bed, the bright stripes of color across the desk top. Other caves to enter, dust to disturb. Anna, the word *disdain,* stairs to climb ever so slowly . . .

The red notebook had begun as fragments, and its shapelessness had frightened Webb. It had been too real. Knowing Anna, knowing himself equal impossibilities. So what could the words do but mirror inadequacy. First the red notebook had contained only his words, but later with an ocean between them, it had gradually been filled by Anna's letters, his answers sent and unsent, his impressionistic meditations and snatches of verse. Webb remembered how seldom he had reread the pages after they were covered with words. Fear again. Anna lost somewhere in the words, himself smothered.

I was afraid of words as we had been afraid of crowds. Saying *black woman* and *white man* destroyed Anna and Charles. They would miss cues, botch lines, two novices inept and nervous before an impatient audience. Black and white. Not only losing the stage personality but floundering unanchored to any identity at all.

Did Anna want to die. Did she want to be released from the words. He could not write them. *Black. White.* Instead he preserved fragments. Warmth of bodies. Hands touching. The park and dying leaves. River running brownly. Twilight. Dawn. Shadowy transitions. And he did not reread. Did not try to order or make whole. Young man's words that were disguise as much as discovery.

He knew one day he would repudiate them. Hate them. For their fear, the lie of Anna.

Turning the pages now, drowsy with age, with the room's ancient familiarity, with words and words written since the red notebook had been laid aside, Webb felt time and distance collapse. That last summer on the riverbank she fed me grapes. We watched the emerald-headed ducks glide past trailing their dun mates and children. She said you have not forgiven and I looked away, tried to focus on the far shore, the sailboats and racing sculls. Wanting her so much, so near, all of her within me, as her deep black eyes swallowed my image. A moment the notebook should hold, should balance and preserve. But how in words. I spit seeds on the grass and she leaned backward, black hair a frame, eyes risen to white clouds and blue sky. She was beautiful and I knew I should lean down and press my lips against hers. Here on this bright, summer day. River, sky, trees and grass and sun.

Her words defined my hesitation. She said no one can learn to forgive because forgiveness can't wait. Like a lie. You know at the instant you are asked if forgiveness is truly given. All you can learn later is that perhaps you should have forgiven. She was up on her elbows again, hair dripping almost to the grass, her face still slanted to the sky. She said that's why I don't think we can forgive them and I'm sure they won't forgive us.

He would not read on. Not try to remember. The young man's vision betrayed itself. The constant irony of the thing withheld cruelly revealing all in its absence. Words an elaborate masquerade defining the wearer with more precision than his naked skin. The young man was a pedant, a liar, a fool, he was ignorant, illogical, afraid, and Webb's list grew as he had read, but in spite of these defects, or perhaps because of them, Charles Webb envied the young man. What was the final most difficult fact to accept had been that just as a saint's clairvoyance rested ultimately on his belief in God, the young man's vision had a still center which gave

89

his words a transcendent authenticity—his love of Anna. Nothing Webb had written since had captured that reality.

May was the month in which he had received Anna's last letters.

Dearest,
Please do not be angry with me for taking so long to write. I know it has been a long time because I count in my heart each hour of each day we are apart. You are probably smiling because you think I'm telling a silly lie or that I'm just silly. But I'm telling the truth. More times than I can keep track of, a thought filled with you drops down like a cloud and covers me. Not a dark, unpleasant cloud, but gentle and caressing like your hands over my skin. For a moment I'm lost to what's around me. I actually begin to float upward, lifted by my dream of you. Then some lifeless detail, a word or object suddenly cries out that it exists, that I must turn and pay attention. But in a way, I suppose I'm grateful for the petty details that accumulate to fill my days. Time would be unbearable if I had to remain suspended between the dream of you which rushes so close to being real and the distant reality of your presence which remains unmoved by my desire.

This seems so little to send after such a long while. But soon we will talk forever. You'll get sick of all the things I have to say. You'll want me to keep quiet. Aw Shut up! you'll say in exasperation when I tell you for the thousandth time I love you.

Anna,
I fear the very intensity of our love. From the distance of a year its heights seem unattainable, the day to day reality of its existence in words, things and actions is lost beneath a golden aura of recollection. The idea of being with Anna again is just as impossible to conceive as the lonely void had been before we were separated. Your image of perfection, the rhythms and emotions it revives have broken away from the limitations of particular individuals, times, and places. It is no longer the love

of Charles and Anna, but *love,* a sublime, universalized condition that no one can approach or call his own. Being here, I can't help thinking of Proust, of Swann and his Odette. So you and I won't be able to shut our eyes and will into being our former love because that love or more importantly its transfigured image can only exist in our minds. To myself I admit all these things, reaching and dismissing countless stages of sobering skepticism and somber faith. Not enough can be said, and there is nothing to be said. Battered between these alternatives I also find it increasingly difficult to write. What has been spontaneous, self-justifying, has become for me an enormous crisis of will power, a labored, compulsory task for which I have neither words nor spirit.

Dearest,

There has been a long silence. By far the longest of all. I could not stand still, Charles. I have been growing. But more of me goes into this letter than ever climbed the stairs to Billy's room. Past the smell of onions, salami and burnt grease, the step somewhere in the middle that groaned and threatened to swallow me. Always dark, voices, sometimes the jukebox of the sandwich shop beneath Billy's room. Why after the party was over, and being taken home did I say yes. It was late, I was tired. No special attraction. Had we danced at the party? That I couldn't recall. But he offered a ride home and late and rather than walk lots of us piled in but finally just Billy and I so I said for some reason though I was tired and had barely seen his face yes I would stop.

How many times did I go there? Would it be better to say once, to be able to say just once and I was weak and please forgive. Or should I say to you to whom I must be able to say everything: that I went back, learned to rely upon those trips to Billy's room, learned to stop questioning each button undone, each layer of reserve melted in his arms. That I learned to stop torturing myself, buried the guilt and shame. Would you understand.

Please come home this summer as you promised. I will be here, I will be yours in a new way, I believe a deeper and fuller way. I will have changed and you will have changed. It will be a new beginning; it can be the start of our forever.

Answer (not sent)

The key is her handwriting. She can adopt various types of handwriting just as she can choose and sustain the disguise of a life style. What I have always been uncertain of was the number of removes each one of her poses put her from the truth. Now I know the problem is and will always be that her conception of the truth consists only of the sum total of perspectives contributed by her styles. There is no layer which cannot be peeled away either by me or someone else. There is no fundamental reserve that cannot be disturbed. Each pose has some corner of the truth, but no point exists at which the discreet units form a unity. When Anna has wished to be the satirical correspondent, up popped material upon which she could exercise her wit and spite. When she was depressed, enough of the chaos weighed upon her, enough of the world's cruelty and emptiness blunted her sensibilities to justify the most severe stoic meditations. Her desire for a new dress, her concern for her figure, her hair, stray cats, children allowed her to launch unashamedly into the most feminine epistles. Each slot, each pose that could be validated, verified on its own terms made the gathering of the whole implausible, the effort of consolidation and appraisal less urgent. In fact as she had gradually realized she could withhold, could crowd out the inevitable evaluation indefinitely. That part of her, that life which included another man, his bed and the lovers' hours they spent together had for her no more relevance than any other of the lives she had lived. And it could be, she decided, the last of which I learned. Perhaps I would have never learned.

Another letter to be added. Twenty-five years and his hand must copy out Anna's words, end the story in the red notebook:

You came but didn't stay. You made love to me as you would to a whore. But that didn't matter. You couldn't stay for long, we couldn't continue looking past each other's eyes each time our bellies were stuck together. And though it was not love, we created what love might create, what only love should be allowed to bring into the world. Your son is a young man now. Today I told him your name. He knew many things about you before that. The better part of you, what we once shared. But I am dying. I can neither lie nor leave certain things incomplete. The boy should not be left with shadows, with rents in his past. It will be up to him to pull the pieces together. I have been fair. Of you he knows more good than evil. But of course that is meager fairness, perhaps the greatest unfairness to you both. I know I will not live out the year. The doctors are honest and fair. Sometimes I wish I had followed you, had put my life in your hands. Surely the bitterness passed off. Surely your wound healed of itself, and you remembered more of me than the transgression of that stranger to us both, my flesh.

I cannot visualize you any more. Sometimes I pretend to see you in him, but that trick is shoddy. He has never known you so the most important things, what I would want to see, could not be transferred, reborn. And you haven't even known he existed. You chose the kind of break we made and I respected your choice, your right. Perhaps I should have sent a picture or his name, revealed his existence before now. But I was waiting for a moment when everything inside me would be calm, detached, entirely distinct from any memory of you and our love. I see now I have waited for death. I believe someday he will try to find you.

Semana Santa was ending. Tonight the final procession bearing *Cristo Negro* would weave through the warm, spring night drawing behind it a brown cleansing river of gypsies through the streets of Málaga. The evening like others for Webb would begin with cocktails under the awning of a café, with the small boys who knelt beside you to find their faces in your shoes. Webb would sit and observe, then stroll along café lined streets to be observed. Simply a matter of time. God in his abundance would provide fuel for every fire.

Webb did not live until those first moments in the street, until the tartness of the iced gin brought sudden clarity and amplification to his senses, until he was certain again that everything he felt was real and would die. From the glassed in terrace of his hotel, he had watched the first night's festivities unfold. His moment of certainty had not come. Perhaps it was the harsh lighting and round tables with their drooping skirts of immaculate glowing linen. Perhaps he lacked all assurance because he sat alone at his table against a back wall able to see only the top of the lighted fountain which sprang from the main square below.

He could arouse no enthusiasm that first night for the seemingly endless courses brought by his white-jacketed waiter. Around Webb the other diners had seemed spurred on, first by the canned music provided by the management, then by the carnival enthusiasm of the band playing below in the square. Silverware clattered against china, metal lids of warming dishes reverberated like tympanum, talk was vociferous, laughter exploded between mouthfuls. Through the glass wall Webb could see the harbor, a cluttered pattern of masts illuminated against the blackness of the sea. Closer, blinking from color to color through a pastel spectrum, the crown of a fountain swayed unsteadily in the air. Gradually the room dimmed and emptied till Webb, who had moved to a table beside the glass, and his waiter, a blur and a red dot as he stood smoking in a corner beside the bar, were the sole occupants.

–*Uno más, por favor*, Webb asked the darkness, vaguely guilty because he knew he was keeping the waiter overtime, preventing the man from joining the crowd down in the street. The sentinel moved slowly, ice from a bucket like bones cracking, the musical bumping of cubes against glass walls. The drink was set down. In the man's face Webb could see no anger, no expectation or impatience. What the night might mean to him, the singing, dancing, the women in the streets, did not reach his eyes, was as concealed as his opinion of the drink he served his last customer. The man may prefer to be here, to be earning the large tip I must leave, to be avoiding the noise, the confusion below. Webb preferred to believe that, but either way desired some sign from the man, something beyond neutral passivity that would spell out an explicit relationship between them, define it so it could be forgotten, no longer intrude. The waiter's restaurant English and Webb's tourist Spanish, however, made the possibility of spoken understanding remote, and the waiter withheld from his features and gestures any expressive movement. When and how he had finally risen from his seat at the window, Webb didn't know, but in something that seemed like a dream he remembered the body of a young sailor that was somehow the body of the waiter, and the white waiter's jacket that somehow had become part of a blue naval uniform whose brass buttons embossed with anchors were being undone by Webb's hands to kiss the cold, saltiness of drowned flesh beneath.

The last day Webb boarded the crowded bus for Torremolinos. A seventeen mile bus trip down the coast took over an hour; the delapidated vehicle made innumerable stops picking up anyone, anywhere along its route, fortunate enough to make themselves seen in the roadside clutter and dust. To Webb it seemed impossible that the sea could be less than a mile away paralleling their route. No breeze penetrated the dust. In the sunlight's glare Webb imagined he could see the tightly packed layers of dust and air forming a solid, inert mass through which the rumbling bus must plunge. The engine wheezed and sputtered straining its dust clogged lungs on the slightest grade or when it lurched into motion again after picking up another clot of peasants, the brown peasants Webb saw as forlorn, indistinguishable from one another or from the dusty loads which they carried. The occupants of the bus were silent; only the animals slowly suffocating within the press of human bodies muttered weakly their sounds of terror and distress.

Webb could not stand still. Like the others who had boarded too late for a seat he was jostled violently as the bus careened headlong over the rutted highway. Since he was taller than most of the passengers his drunken motions were more visible. After each particularly vicious thrust, Webb would find some dark face staring intently at him as if the white man had caused the collision and directed its force. But before the eyes could trap him Webb and the accuser were driven apart just as suddenly as they had met. Webb knew, unlike him, the Spaniards who filled the bus carried no comforting images of sudden relief once the bus reached its destination. They saw no expanse of cool, blue sea, no golden sands stirred by breezes coming in off the water. They would walk away from the beach and the lush resort hotels that fronted it, toward the shantytown that hid itself from the gleaming island of shops, banks, and restaurants. Their eyes told Webb he was an intruder. Asked why they could not be left alone, why even here they must be reminded that nothing is theirs, not even this hot cramped space that carries them from one job to another. Webb realized he was offending them, that in his blue cord suit and madras tie he should have taken a taxi between the two towns, a vehicle that preserved the necessary *détente* between two alien forms of life.

As if to cut off his escape, to fuse the passengers into one unnatural whole, a new wave of heat dropped like a blanket around the bus. Webb wanted to take off the jacket that lapped against his skin like a wet rag, but such an extravagant movement was impossible to arms pinned at his sides. The pools of moisture that had formed in every cavity of his body began to overflow and crawl like insects inside his clothes. His eyelids dripped and blurred his vision. If he could have seen the floor of the bus, he wouldn't have been surprised to find puddles forming around his shoes. He was in kindergarten again, his face on fire, unable to move from his seat while the other children laughed and pointed at the pale liquid spreading beneath his desk.

The bus had slowed, finally coming to a complete stop when a flock of goats being driven toward the sea blocked the highway. A thousand collar bells began their high-pitched jingling, delicate goat feet clattered against asphalt. Webb looked down on the black and white wave of animals driven past the front of the bus. Their tiny horns were frozen ripples in the bobbing surface of lean backs and pointed heads. Sitting cross-legged on a donkey the leering shepherd appeared unnatural because no tuft of beard sprouted from his chin or horns from his forehead. With the racket and dust came the rancid smell of the animals, detaching itself, inundating the bus until it harmonized with the garlic, olive oil, excrement, and sweat that reigned in concert.

Webb shut his eyes, wished for some means to deprive all his senses just as abruptly. The bus was motionless less than a minute, the herd of goats did not contain all the goats in the world, but for Webb the moment was an eternity. He was tossing in his bed, feverish, unable to sleep. Distance drone of heavy bombers, the apocalypse thick in their bellies. Anna weeping. *Too late. Too late.*

The engine coughed and jerked raggedly into life. One last straggling black kid bolted past the wheels and the bus clambered again toward Torremolinos.

The Tower of the Mills. From Barcelona southward the coast was dotted with what had once been Roman military outposts, then fishing villages, and finally emblems of the good life in the sun that brought French, Germans, Swedes,

Dutch, Englishmen, and Americans streaming to sun, ocean, sand, cheap living, and each other. Pedrigaleho, Castelldefels, Sitges, Tarragona, Málaga, Marbella. The view always the same. A stretch of white sand, the shimmering blue of the ocean, a modern high-rise hotel flanked by the perpetual construction of a newer, bigger, brighter, more lavish accommodation. From Paris there are six flights daily to the Costa Brava and the Costa del Sol. Webb remembered the brochures, the posters, the fresh tans of the clerks in the travel agency. Champs Élysées. No, it didn't matter that he wasn't a Frenchman, still eligible for all cut rates, discounts, package deals, I know just the thing . . . it's a lovely . . .

From the square Webb walked down a narrow street crowded with restaurants and bars. Signs were usually trilingual, English, German, French, and sometimes Spanish last, inviting the stroller to eat, drink, wear, smell, hear, feel, possess what was displayed in windows or walk through the low doorways covered by swaying strings of beads and submit to the lure of darkness on the other side of thick cool walls. The paved street became rutted, then gravel, and finally earth packed tight by the passage of countless feet. A crumbling stone balcony overlooked the beach, and twisting down from this platform a staircase even more dilapidated than the decayed landing was cut into the rock. Webb could see figures moving beneath him, two-way traffic slowly negotiating the steep weather-beaten stairs. Scrawny children, dark ragamuffins with stylized saucer eyes played on the staircase, skipped along its precarious edges, and scrambled over sharp, broken rocks. A group would swirl by Webb's legs, threatening to topple him, or in a tangle of arms and legs plunge them together helplessly down the stairs. At many of the landings, cut deeper into the less solid rock or constructed of an incredible variety of odds and ends on outcroppings, what must be the homes of these gypsy children came into view. Webb could discern no possibility of ventilation or light in these warrens, only the scooped out entranceways like drooling mouths, littered with refuse and filth. Occasionally a shriveled old woman or one nursing a child too young to climb the rock staircase would be squatting at their holes. They smiled toothless smiles as the children's bright eyes smiled, even muttered wearily some automatic greeting as the children always sang out when strangers passed. Webb could not put his hand into his pocket, felt ashamed of what he would draw out. The sea breeze had begun to refresh him and at every other turning of the staircase he could see crackling with sunlight the ocean spread across the horizon.

Webb walked along the beach dreaming a Prufrock dream of himself. Semana Santa was almost over. Málaga would become a staid city of cautious, middle-class Spaniards, and Torremolinos would shed its spring skin of faces for the summer crowd. Nights would become as hot as the days and the days too long. The endless gin tonic of an afternoon would flow.

Webb dreamed of a young man. Saw not sandals tied over his feet but bare flesh, from the tough soles of his feet curling in the hot sand to the strip of black cloth that hugged his narrow hips. His bronzed legs naked and strong, pounding the sand in a sudden dash to the surf as their power lifted him high into the air, bounding, floating till the cool water rose with a shock against his chest. The playful fight with the sea until he was no more than a black dot seen from the shore.

Webb removed his sandals, rolled his trousers to the knee and padded along the damp sand. He had stuffed his tie in the breast pocket of his cord suit jacket slung over his shoulder, and his white batiste shirt was open to the waist. The sea was a dull roar in his brain; water lapped against his ankles coolly, rhythmically. Slowly the sand was sucked away from under his toes, the imprint they made pushing deeper into the strand. Webb stared at the brilliant sea, the subtle bands of color descending toward the horizon, tried to locate the points where green became blue and blue purple. But the play of light and atmosphere danced continuously, never allowed his eyes to find end or beginning. A shudder passed through Webb's body. He was aware of the strain on his eyes, of the sand that tugged at his feet, the horizon meeting somewhere behind his back. The damp shirt was clammy against his shoulders, chill, threatening like a sudden draft from an unknown source.

Sea girls combing. Webb back-pedaled carefully placing his feet to avoid the quick foam-edged rushes of water that chased the bottom of his pants. Farther up the beach a low white building painted in hulking red letters across its front *Bar Genymar*. A cluster of red and white umbrellas promised service outdoors, a shaded chair facing the sea, an iced drink. He would come.

Too many bodies littered the sand. Webb picked his way, erratic, cautious like a crab scuttling among the flesh mounds. He chose a table closest to the sea and sat half in, half out of the shadow of its striped umbrella. The gin was called Green Fish, was raw and cloying, made Webb tremble as the first long gulp settled unsteadily in his stomach. For the first time that day he allowed himself to ask questions, to have a past. To ask what future that past implied. Gin said you are an old man. And tired the old man replied. Place names came to him, automatic, insinuating, a list he had been forced to memorize and must always upon demand be prepared to repeat. From the tall glass fumes, incense rising. Dream of Anna in the White Mountains. A steep green hill. We tumble down, accelerating as body pitches over and over within the earth carpet unfurling. Wind whips the high grass, hisses, falling we land in a heap. We are alone. Beneath the sea. We are its creatures. Green hills, deep caves, always a seascape where the land flattens into blue distance and the eye can go no farther. Said to be the lair of the dragon. Benign now, turned to stone, baking in the sun. Wind whips. Her shaggy sweater is covered with dry grass, straw clings to her black hair. Smiling she whips, her fingers comb. Blackness floats. I see it spread against a pillow. A hand smooths it, touches her dark face. She is beneath me. The long strands are wind. I bury my face in the black wind. She begins to cry.

Her son would say to her the white man never loved you. Her son would say I loved only my words about her. My son would say I loved nothing. He would find notes to him written in her books, notes that were written while he was still a baby, even before he was born, while she carried him, she would have begun a record believing someday that if he read the books she had loved and saved he would understand. She would write the story of her love, her submission, her trust and belief. And how when she was loved no more, she had let me leave without a word. He would know she had given everything to me, that I had touched greatness only when I touched her and that when she died I still didn't understand, didn't have the faintest idea of what had been given, what had been lost. That he had been lost. He would know I had lied. That my paintings, music, and books were a monument of lies, deceit. He is my son. What I had planted in her black flesh. He had no name. Over her body I will offer him my name, but he will spit on the floor and laugh, louder and louder. Then he will say . . .

The voice was Al's, rousing him, shattering the mirror.

—Hail Charles, full of gin. Blessed art thou among men for Albert has found you. Wrinkled and puckered into a second grotesque face Al's naked belly hung flabby-jawed over skimpy red trunks. The red hairs of his chest, bleached and curled, were incandescent.

—Why did you leave me, Charlie. And come back without a word. I was worried sick. Above the shaggy beard his smile arched to his ears.

—What a lucky break this is. Dammit. I was nearly going nuts with worry so I decided to get some sun and sea. They relax me you know. Nothing like being near the sound of the surf at night. Whales own lullaby. I'm snoring in a minute and sleep all night just like a baby. You know what I mean?

From the sea a squealing girl was lifted. Two hands clasped her waist momentarily suspending her above the billowing breakers while she screamed louder and thrashed perfect bronzed legs. The hands ducked her again in an explosion of foam.

Webb knew his voice would falter if he attempted to speak immediately. He took the plump hand held out toward his, wagging as it wagged, accepting its presence as he did the image of his dying body each morning in the mirror.

—I won't ask you why, Albert. I'm not prepared to listen and I doubt that I would understand what you would call reasons. I won't ask why, just how, how did you find me.

—You might say I didn't look. Just went about my own business and—poof—here we are, face to face.

—Did you follow me?

—Let's drop it, Charlie. A coincidence is a coincidence. Don't you know I got better things to do than dog you.

—It's simple of course. You've seen him. And we waited here last year. Almost exactly to the day. Where else would I be. And you. The vulture . . . just minding his own business. Just hanging black in the sky. His own business.

—Now wait, Charlie . . . wait. You're going a bit hard. I got feelings too. His bulk swallowed the chair. Like some part of Al already digested and organic, the metal legs he straddled propelled his lobster body closer to the table where Webb sat.

—Look here, *señor*. There is hardly any sense in which I'm

an outsider in this. I cry like you do when we don't fine him. I cry and spend the blood money, not one peseta into the sea where I promise myself it will all go. Just because you feel so damned bad is no reason to believe all the grief in the world belongs to you. I cry, Charlie. I figure you came here to mourn. My eyes tell me at least that. If you'd open your windows you'd see Al is a mourner too. And that other thing. The sting . . . remorse.

Al's face disintegrated into broken spirals of color and motion through the bottom of the tall glass as Webb drained the last of his silver gin. What did it matter Webb asked himself. Here we are again. This fat, red-bearded man and myself. Both ridiculous, both obscene. It was laughable afterall. The classic pair, umbilically joined. The knight dragging his squire across endless plains of La Mancha. But who is who. Which one the deluded fanatic.

–Charlie, I hope you're listening. Al leaned forward, digging the legs of his chair deeper into the sand. His tone was measured now, his voice calm, conciliatory. After calling for drinks he folded the ham hands on the round tabletop.

–There seems to me something you're not willing to admit. Like it or not we're in this together, and when I say *in* I mean from the bald soles of our feet to the toppest headhair. You think the boy will come, don't you. You think too that maybe all these years he has been hiding from you, or leastways from something you caused. All what I say is true, ain't it, Charlie?

Webb's answer was half a nod, a barely perceptible downward dipping of his head toward the sweating glass of gin.

–And if the boy is disgusted, lost, or scared you did it, didn't you? You made him into whatever he was, if he was anything. But if we don't find him I gotta face the failure too, don't I? It ain't something you can do alone. In fact you don't have the right to do it alone. We'll go back to

103

town together. We'll wait together. The rod and the staff. That's the way it has to be, it has to be this way, Charlie. And Charlie . . . Cecil ain't coming. He ain't coming to meet you. He's going home, Charlie. I sent him home. He won't be here, Charlie.

—I had so much I wanted to tell him. And now, here, we would have time; so much time. Do you know what's happening, Albert? I am an old man, I am dying, Albert. Tell me he is coming that I am not dying. That Anna . . .

—Hail Albert full of grace.

Hail Albert full of grace.

Hail Albert. Hail Albert.

—Come on Charlie, the night is young. The shoeshine pimps are just hitting the streets. Let's get a good shine, Charlie. And give them a fabulous tip. Let's get good brandy and sip under the umbrellas. The show will be pretty as it always is. Loud, wild night show for us. Let's get away from here. Maybe buy a new tie or a kerchief or something bright. Feel different in new things, in bright new things. Come on the night's so young.

The woman was arrayed in purple and scarlet, and bedecked with gold and jewels and pearls, holding in her hand a goblet of bronze brandy in which she dipped her lips then I my lips then she anointed her fingers and with fingers she wet my member and the short curly hairs perfumed with Felipe Segundo. Onto my back I settled received by the blood-red bedspread as I would be by a mother's lap. Soft and drifting my peace was such I could float any place I pleased, to Paris, to Rome, back to those cities in America, forward to the deep couch of earth in which I would sleep forever. Estrella, whore that she was, had no scruples concerning my brandy letch and seemed either drunk herself or wooed into a compatible urge because she alternately wet and licked my liquorish stick with a rhythm neither hurried nor mechanical, a slow baptism of damp fingertips dragged lightly the whole length, quick dabs at my scrotum and body hair, then the languor of her tongue undoing the lubrication or to be more precise supplying a new balm from her moist lips. I watched her. When she moved it was on all fours, crouched like a beast. She would drag the tops of her thin breasts over my naked flesh. Her body was neither voluptuous nor skinny. It had to be both: meaty round buttocks, drooping pear breasts thin till the pendulous diamond-tipped bulbs that scratched parallel lines into my skin. Estrella. Al did not exaggerate when he sang your skills, five nights waiting for Webb and five different women you were for me. And this last meeting, this slow removal of all of Cecil through the tube at which you drink reveals a lore in you Estrella old as memory as old as lonely men in cities, ancient craft passed down through generations like the concourse Egyptians had with the dead, how they could preserve, make lifelike, extract the brain through a nostril just as you exquisitely diminish me through my root's blind eye.

World must have stopped hours ago. I listen and hear only your breathing, the lapping of waves on a shore thousands of planets away. Life must end after stillness like this. Not simply my life in time but all the tumult and clamor in the streets, the jungles, the seas. Surely a judgment has been brought upon the earth with this revelation. The blood of all the saints and martyrs ready to burst from my groin.

Dawn came. I am undeceived. Dawn of the last day, always comes again or tomorrow or however you perceive of never-ending. We stand naked at the window. Madrid sleeps below us, gray, misty, undisturbed except for the whining of motor bikes, the waspy, angry buzz of machines as unhappy as their masters at being routed out to thump

105

along the empty, early city streets. My hand goes around her waist. Fingers spread concave at the deep indentation. So here we are Estrella, the last two. A new beginning. Sounds you hear are machines so accustomed to early rising and hitting the streets that they perpetuate the ritual although their masters are no more. Or perhaps it was machines that dragged men from their warm beds. A new beginning. Sons and daughters from your loins. The first few will be indeterminate, kaleidoscopic leavings of many men from many nations, amalgamated children we will welcome but finally the all clear and I can begin to sow a new generation. Adam to Zachariah, Alice to Zenobia. We naked two framed in this dusty window seven stories above wet Madrid. We will name one Webb, for mystery and cunning and the past. Pola, Hans, Martine, Xavier, Carlos, Ingrid, Karl, Vladimir and name after name but do not think Simon.

I pull her closer, fingers in the rib grooves. A cage I could shatter if I squeezed with all my strength, brittle curving bone, her narrow waist. But I relax and let my hand drop, curl it round toward me, past the softness of her flank, the molded contour of belly to springy hair. She is humming. How far away is the city. How dead.

We turn from the window and our eyes meet, her whore eyes and mine bloodshot, raw. I think the gray dawn light is a blessing, a conspirator because we hold the glance an unnecessary instant and the cracked lips of her whore's mouth soften to a smile.

She is padding a step or two away yet far enough for me to take in all the incongruous body. Emaciated in shank and back and shoulders, two lumps of rump which jiggle giddily on the bone with each step. Straight rail of body which breaks at knees and deep waist to kneel as if in supplication but down farther beast on all fours rummaging beneath the red skirt of the bed cover. Surprising the breadth of beam in one who standing has boyish hips but spread they do to matron amplitude. I bend too and tug the sprig of beard exposed at hemisphere's base. She is up like a cat, bird-caging her fingers and feinting plucks at my groin.

—Estrella.

I want to take her by way of her plump buttocks. It is painful, dry and tight. I relent and leave her folded over the edge of the bed. The softest part of a woman, those two cushions on either side the ragged joint. Inside the thigh, but outside the eye. When she is standing, at the bottom curve of the haunch, that momentary fleshy hesitation before thigh sweeps dramatically outward. Cradle in which the life gates purse, tender vale, unfringed yet redolent of the tangled forest.

My love, Estrella, whom I leave to do the bidding of others. To perform for others.

Estrella come. Let us sit our nakednesses together here on this bed. Let us forget that the city is dead, that we are the last two. I memorized a poem once. If you could understand what I'm telling you, if you knew the poem was really a part of your Sacred Book, you would be scandalized, perhaps even turn me away. But we speak different languages, so if I recite quietly, solemnly, the words will be just so much billing and cooing, particularly if I punctuate the verses with caresses, kisses, even come to a full stop between stanzas so I can dip quickly into you. But no, listen. Let me go all the way through. I'll be selective. Only the most relevant passages, although all of the prophecy is more than appropriate. Such a memorial is the least we can do. A dirge between the pavanes we dance. You stare wonderingly. Perhaps titillated or even bored by the prospect of another sensual game, one more fancy, one more debauchery from my fertile imagination. But no. Relax, cuddle against me while I lean back against this ornate headboard. Is that some astrological sign carved in the center. A sun with stylized, horny rays projected outward. Some creature of the zodiac, a constellation, the universe itself? No, nothing more mysterious than your taste, always poor or bizarre. But we are in mourning. No levity, no tickling of groins, no lip love-making. Just my lips speaking and yours still. The queen is dead.

I will call this farewell or elegy to a dead whore:

And the merchants of the earth weep for her, since no one buys their cargo any more, cargo of gold, silver, jewels and pearls, fine linen, purple, silk and scarlet, cinnamon, spice incense, myrrh, frankincense, wine, oil, flour and wheat, cattle and sheep, horses and chariots and slaves, that is *human souls.*

> The fruit for which thy soul
> longed has gone from thee.
> And all thy dainties and thy
> splendor are lost to thee,
> never to be found again!

> Alas, alas for the great city
> that was clothed in fine linen,
> in purple and scarlet
> bedecked with gold, with jewels
> and with pearls!
> In one hour all this wealth has
> been laid waste.

> Hallelujah! the smoke from her
> goes up for ever and ever.

If I had been wise, a flatterer, Estrella, I might have sung for you the Song of Solomon. Visited your breasts and belly with heaps of metaphor. But you understand that you don't understand so what matter if I speak my farewell bitterly or like a spring morning. I am leaving you and leaving him. Which works out to be the same thing. Unless his story changes radically. Unless he is a Janus in disguise and hides

108

another face beneath that distinguished long white hair. Perhaps one is there, one facing forward, lips I can speak to, that would speak to me. But I cannot take the chance.

One kiss more, a wrestle, a handful of your powder puff and I'll be on my way.

Home

Is always a street on which I happen to be walking. On which to some great extent I am lost as I am lost along this Madrid street.

Little light on the whorizon. Silent distance. I will walk toward that myth of earth touching heaven. As good a destination as any I can perceive, as any revealed to Cecil in this last consultation of his whoroscope. I am drunk and funky.

Behind the jumbled silhouette of buildings a true horizon must stretch. Walk to the edge of the city, to the favella's musty plain. I will gaze far out to the low hills which will be blue as morning light spreads over them. The gypsies will still be sleeping and I will move as stealthy as a dream among them, stepping always closer to that quiet distance.

The whore rising from her bed and I am helpless because I see Esther's bare back and I remember that the nightmare is irresistible that my sleep is troubled more and more by images of Simon scraped from her womb and the horror deceives me so that I must live it believe it feel myself gouging him out from her body. Fantasy of my son dripping into the pot.

But I know I did not kill him, wish him away, that of all things I dared hope for, I was most fearful hoping for him. Esther tried to do too much. Her body was just too tired to carry him any longer. And I followed the law, I slaved as she slaved learning the law. I was learning, learning so much for her and for him. But something broke. He could not wait and I dream I am responsible for his terrible coming. I am masked, a white aproned butcher who drags son from mother while some part of me holds her hand and whispers love.

I did not kill him. Dream is perverse. Perverse as the illusion that somewhere I could lie with my back on the hard ground and have blue sky and clouds against my chest.

Sun is rising and I will shock those eyes I meet in these narrow streets.

Cecil Otis Braithwaite, barrister-at-law, put to sea one day during the spring month of April, 1966. On the hot deck he stood resplendent in loden green, Tyrolean knickers with vest to match aching only for his first glance of Africa. Never did Cecil's wet gaze stray from the opaque screen of soggy atmosphere except to fasten upon the shrieking gulls that hovered over the ferry's stern. The birds were masterful in their lazy glides catching updrafts and currents of sea air that suspended them serenely on lax W's of wing. Unhurriedly, the gulls would dip to scavenge garbage thrown overboard by the stewards. Low over the wàves they skipped like flat stones, nibbling, screeching, beating away competition with rapid flourishes of gull-wing. I too white-bellied and fleet-winged have danced upon the foam sang Cecil to himself. I remember when I was a swan and met this languishing maiden she stroked tender of feathers my long neck and oh so phallic head-piece and it's been so far away I forget now just how we consummated but it was good Cecil blushing lied to himself. If it wasn't me a close friend anyway. Someone took a picture, and though I admit the likeness isn't great, it could be me.

Cecil heard a pig rooting in the narrow companionway where he stood, but when rumbles grew louder and closer and still no fat back in sight, Cecil realized he was hungry.

This here narrow boat carries goats not pig iron he heard Leadbelly explain to the tickee man. Horizon still hid in mist. No green African hills or giraffes visible to Cecil's straining eyes. Algeciras to Ceuta. Someone, a wronged Jew I seem to recall, left the gates open one night to Tarik the Moor, and his band of merry hawks. A bridge here Alexander commanded but ferryman's union stymied the erection which grew no further than huge stones stacked in either edge of the strait. Still to be seen on a clear day when the sea is low. But Cecil saw nothing. Neither weeping Alexander, nor Ilyan weeping in rage, nor the daughter of that wronged Lord of Ceuta weeping in shame, nor Roderic villain weeping for joy while nuzzling his weeper into fat thighs of the Jew's daughter. Cecil heard only gulls scolding and pigs grunting and old wood groan and fart under his feet.

Anisse looked different with her clothes on. Cecil would have preferred that if she had to dress at all, she dressed like a man rather than try to disguise broad, square shoulders, flat chest and backsides beneath the most outrageously feminine frills and flounces. If there was any canon of beauty which vaguely complimented Anisse's physical attributes, Cecil felt it had to be found in plane geometry. Atop Anisse his fantasies had been of surf boards, of sleds, of unknotted pine slats, of flat, honed surfaces scudding his prostate bones. Freckles for breasts, a squared valley between her jutting hipbones. Cecil wanted to sand her. Finish smoothing the tabletop where ribs made slight indentations, and plane away lumps on either side of the navel. Anisse redolent of mothballs and gin raises high one straight ankle and slips boot through the first rail. Like the sea her inner thigh is blue veined. Cecil turns out the light and God is merciful. The flaunted thigh, young again in darkness, shies from its mate till compass spreads to an angle of eighty-four degrees. Limber at last, the forked tongue engages Cecil in earnest conversation.

–I grow old, I grow old, should I eat my sausage rolled or pat it into patties.

Cecil tries to remember how to answer a question. The process is too difficult. Better if I just keep quiet and listen.

–I thought one day I would just stop. You know what I mean. Just have no more urge. The natural conclusion of a natural process. I hoped that as I lost all power to attract, I would no longer be attracted to attracting. But Rome wasn't crushed in a day; it fell into gradual disrepair. And I despaired over regretting over loss over obsolescence over gyres that cycled me phased me out. I feared a rocking chair, a porch on long summer evenings alone, I feared drool and difficult bowels, despair. . . .

She is not flirting—she is climbing the rail. Cecil stirred from reverie fuzzily considers the possibility of action. A board balanced on its edge, she has been swaying there an hour. The boa goes. She goes. Cecil squeals barely audible above the wind, *Stop, don't jump,* but Anisse is already shriveling from sea cold. Cecil, too, is suddenly salty-eyed as he dreams of Anisse sea changed, scaly and supple-tailed, of hair growing and her chicken voice gone to pure nightingale. Anisse rock candy calling over the sea come and get it.

There is no Africa. Only curtain mist and sea split by prow. Cecil is afraid to approach the rail. A tiny man with a big mouth screams *Man overboard. Man overboard,* inside Cecil's chest. Through the spiraling echoes a pig roots for food. Cecil will not release the voice because Cecil knows, in spite of her freckles and plains, Anisse is not a man but a woman, and in spite of the fact that she is a woman, she doesn't want to dance at the end of any more hooks.

Salt sea. Smell of vinegared privates floating in brine.

Metal sea stairs narrow and unsteady Cecil winds from upper to middle deck and into the ship's bar. He is tired of waiting for Africa, for gulls to speak. He is asked for a cigarette. No burnoose but Arab nevertheless who is close to Cecil's face and whose smoke lightly expelled is a warm shadow on Cecil's cheek. I am taller than the Arab and I speak better English. Cecil nods as the man puffs and emits English in a throaty, French-spotted phlegm of regrets, losses, orotund hopes. He is the prodigal returning; he will be welcomed, understood, loved, be a man again. The Arab explains how cold the foreigners were and how greedy. The back of an Arab hand wipes an Arab nose. Cecil's brandy comes and for a moment he believes they are sinking, that sea crawls darkly over the portholes. A lurch makes glass tinkle against his teeth. My teeth are better than his. The Arab has been away many years, but still he knows a man who does wonderful things with foreign currency, who does not exchange but multiplies dollars, pounds, and French francs into stacks of Moroccan dirhams. Just give him my name. Do not trust the others. They are robbers, cold, greedy.

Another cigarette, tent folds, and Arab glides away. Son of Allah. Of Africa too, but I seek the black kings. Andalus. Ilyan smiling promised Roderic: *I will never feel satisfied until I bring thee such hawks as thou never sawest in thy life.* Tarik avenger came giving his name to a rock. A country with delightful valleys and fertile lands, rich, watered by many large rivers and abounding in springs of sweetest water. Lime trees, lemon trees, and most of the fruits of earth grow in all seasons, and the crops succeed one another without interruption.

Some say it is a triangle of land. Some say it is the tail of a bird, a peacock's tail lush-eyed and brilliant. Others are silent upon the matter, but spread themselves darkly over the land building mighty towers, abstract, geometrical forms within whose ramparts there are gardens and vaulted ceilings of crystal. The land provides and we straddle it as we do our horses, our women.

So Cecil crosses the sea to see where it all came from. He has cleansed himself. Expiated his sins by committing fornication within the dry husk of an old woman. He has promised to wash his hands and feet, to cry out impurities from his eyes before he touches the African soil. If it were allowed, he would plant himself in the sand. Stand like a flag that claims possession, satisfied to be forever possessed. I am part of it. It is part of me. The closer I draw, I realize how impossible all else was, how all that past melts like a wax casing as I am nearer and nearer the flame.

When I left this land, I rode a white horse, my beard was thick and my sword studded with jewels. Then I was a doctor; I looked to the stars and learned all manner of things of mind and body, but with the rest I remembered fear. Then I took to tinkering. I made swords and countless, ingenious toys. Though I built on a larger scale at times, I began to keep a garden and learned to cook. *Matamoros* came on a white horse and pitched me from the land. I was herded into ships which my blood propelled, and I was sold as chattel in another world. I had no garden and after their rutting time even my women laughed. I worked harder than I should have just so I could sleep. In the end I learned to sleep while awake. They called me night.

Sea sways, curdling where ship slices its wound across the strait. Algeciras to Ceuta. Iago matador goads the black bull. The moment has come, and somehow the silence of the vast crowd, the sudden intensity of the sun leaning closer to the arena, the light glinting from specks of blood dotting the pink sand, the matador's conspiring smile inform even the bull of the moment's arrival. Toro knows. He would bellow, but the sword is too close, too real. Under the sun he is wax melting.

114

Felipe Segundo. A religious fanatic. A collector of Bosch. A moralist who kept the Tabletop of the Seven Deadly Sins in his bedroom. A king of Andalus, the Netherlands, and the New World. A brandy to the waiter who served Cecil and knew none of these things. *Cinco pesetas.* Down the mothering hatch. Mouth not eyes the soul hole. Word made flesh made liquid made Cecil's guts cringe as gulping all three ounces he hurriedly secreted one more revelation. El Moro. Sons of hambone where you been? To a bar-b-que. Pig bones roasted and toasted, juicified with hot mustard ketchup pepper salt tabasco sugar onion pickle soul sauce. I got the shit all over my white shirt and under my fingernails.

—So this cat said to me *Work in your garden.* Well you know what I told the mother. You know where I told the Malcolm Frazer to go.

—So this big, tough-looking fag jumped up from the table and just like he was in full drag leans over and in a high, squeaky voice says if you don't like it, you can kiss my pussy.

Soul hole. Cecil would find a job in Constance Beauty's straightening parlor. Cecil would make it. Jive his way through one set of real and one set of false teeth. Cecil had been a singer, a dancer, a cop. Cecil had bootlegged and pushed shit, played a little semi-pro basketball and baseball, even got to Florida one year with the Dodgers before a near fatal indiscretion with one lighter and brighter than himself almost ended all careers. Cecil had been a bank clerk, a high school teacher, and had sold Watkin's products before finally finding the law. They had just laid the cornerstone of that new office so long in coming when Cecil retired from the service of the Lord. Justice.

—No, I don't know much about hairdressing, Miss Constance, but I have good hands and a strong mind and I'm willing to learn.

—Well it coulda been worse, Sister Esther. He coulda started workin for Process Pete where all them sissies and hoodlums go.

The narrow ship plies backward and forward relentlessly.

Duty free so Cecil took a bottle for himself and remounted the corkscrew twists of staircase. Clearer now. Veins of blue wider in the sea. At first blinking in the sunlight and spray Cecil couldn't decide whether Africa rolled across the horizon or was just some cloud of fog and mist being pushed seaward from the land. Behind him Spain and Europe had disappeared. From the bow white water churned outward in undulating waves. As sky brightened the sea became a tabletop crowded with glistening crystal and silver. Cecil hadn't asked her to come and for each other they hadn't done much, but in a sudden surge of sensibility and regret, after tilting it to his lips, he tossed overboard the half empty bottle of Felipe Segundo and hoped the sea would carry it in the right direction.

3

. . . We consist of everything the world consists of, each of us, and just as our body contains the genealogical table of evolutions as far back as the fish and even much further, so we bear everything in our soul that once was alive in the soul of men. Every god and devil that ever existed . . .

—HERMAN HESSE
Demian

WITH THE AID OF A POCKETBOOK EDITION OF
Webster's *New World Dictionary* Esther Braithwaite began
her memoirs:

All alibis are anonymous. Any act allows arbitration
among antagonists. After admitting accidents, amorality
advances. An axiom assures acquittal although adversity at-
tacks antecedents. Africa awaits. Before babies babble battles begin. Boiling blood builds bastions. Battering behe-
moths besiege bulwarks. Brawling bunches board boats.
Cruisers, canoes, corsairs, clippers carry crowds. Crazed
children cry continually, cough catarrh. Caesar ceases cutting cheese. Decrees: Denizens destroy. Deserters die. Dis-
senting dregs, drab, dirty, disgust diligent dissuaders. Do
dwarfs dare deceive? Everyone endures education. Eager
egos elucidate entire etymologies. Empty. Easy essays en-
slave. Electricity emits energy, earnestness enacts ennui.
Encourage excitement. Everybody errs even famous fakers.
From freedom fear forms. Foolishness. Forget free food.
Forge felicity's formulas. Freeze flippancy. Fallacious fan-
fares, fragile faiths fashion fearful foment. Feral fecundity
forever.

Gabriel, God's gadfly, gaily goaded good genitals. Geria-
trics germinate gelded gifts. Gethsemane's ghostly gestation
gores gizzards. Gravestone grass grows greedier gazes
greenly, grinning gulps gristle. Guillotine gypsies. Harass
heathens. Here Heaven hurts, Hell helps. Hurry home,
hurry home.

119

Esther sought the word from Alpha to Omega. Cecil's last chance rested in her hands, but her hands were palsied by ignorance of the word. Cecil must be a saint, join her in the posthumous fire dance or at least that's how she saw what the poet had called fiery, angelic consummation. The death of Cecil in some faraway land had to be put in the proper light, illuminated as the selfless sacrifice of a saint in his foreign mission. Oh Cecil, why did you do it.

Esther practiced. She grew to love the dictionary, and each word was something to fondle and caress, a new life that came into existence when she had copied it out, memorized its meaning, and could add it to the litanies she chanted each night in her bed.

liberal: 1. generous   2. ample; abundant   3. not literal or strict   4. tolerant; broadminded   5. favoring reform or progress. *n.* one who favors reform or progress.

liberal arts: literature, philosophy, language, history, etc., as courses of study.

liberality: 1. generosity   2. broad-mindedness.

liberalize: to make or become liberal.

liberate: to release from slavery, enemy occupation, etc.

Liberia: a country on the West coast of Africa founded by freed U.S. Negro slaves: area, 43,000 sq. mi.; pop. 1,600,000.

libertine: a man who is sexually promiscuous.

liberty: 1. freedom from slavery, captivity, etc.   2. a particular right, freedom, etc.   3. *usually pl.* excessive freedom or familiarity.   4. leave given to a sailor to go ashore.

libidinous: lustful, lascivious.

libido: 1. the sexual urge   2. *in psychoanalysis,* psychic energy generally: force behind all human action.

libra: (L. a balance, pair of scales), the seventh sign of the zodiac.

Style was another problem. Solved by the simple expedient of finding the proper word for the proper place. Esther studied the meaning of *proper* and the meaning of all the words in its definition quite carefully. She even began to study the words used in the definitions of the words that had defined proper, but she stopped because she believed by then that she had learned the meaning of proper.

On the morning of October first, her pen still shaking, but her determination unflinching before her awesome task, Esther began the canonization of her lost husband.

They say love is a many-splendored thing and my Cecil, son of Zion that he was, splendiforated the bounteous goodies of his loving heart universal. He has been in Your service, dear Father, since that first day his eyes opened and his cute, hairy bottom was slapped by good Dr. Stebbins who wore thick glasses and has loved colored people for longer than any of us can remember. He may be departed by now, bless his soul, but it seems proper and fitting such a fine white man and educated to do the medication of the lives of God's children should bring into being Your servant, Braithwaite christened Cecil Otis that long ago but doesn't really seem so day of October 2, 1933.

He was healthy and refined. Such a child that comes but once into the world to parents couldn't help but edify the indulgence and wonder of Mr. and Mrs. Braithwaite. Cecil came late in their union but You move in ways beknownst to Yourself alone so they asked no questions just demonstrated their gratefulness by the tedious care lavished on that crown to their aged heads. Being advanced in age I suppose they could not easily descend to that proliferating, childish world of their only begotten son. Perhaps here began that endemic trait so significant about Cecil and all saints who must find their own lonely paths through life far from beaten tracks and madding crowds. With his milk (not mother's for the paps of Mrs. Braithwaite had long before gone out of production, but formula made from condensed Carnation milk) the infant Cecil must have imbibed the chill of older lives on the gentle downslope along with those childish dreams that have characterized him since. Faunlike, unresolved, Cecil must have felt that languor of being two so well epitomized in the French by the poet. Half-playful boy, half-goatish old man fearing for his powers but with still something left neither he nor I am, was or will be quite sure of.

I find this section of Your servant's life entangled with skeins of my own eden of early existence. I am tempted even here to anticipate that twined destiny You ordained in Your all-seeing wisdom. I was one of many, but I, too, was a child of old age born twelfth and last to a humble preacher and his second wife. I struggled to orient myself between two worlds, and not seeing the light took on the prancing, coltish ways of the children because beneath the somber black coat of my father, and behind those stiff shirt fronts ironed hard by my mother I did not sense the infinite music of Your presence. They were good people as You well know, and I am only sorry I do not have that choice again, a chance to walk with those good old people today. And so You saw fit to use the same mold twice, shaped my clay and Cecil's with the pattern of Your fond intentions.

I am distressed when I find how little I know of these early days of Cecil's voyaging in the world. From what reports and witnesses I can gather he was on the surface then just as he was till the last moments to eyes not privy to the secrets of Your grand designs—ordinary. But there is a *look*, an almost imperceptible aura of being in the world but not of the world which radiates its effulgence like a halo to other initiates. In my despondency, in the weakness of my flesh, it was to this ghostly radiance that I looked. I would watch him sleeping, pine away in my secret bowels for his touch, for a word. But in the time of my direst need, when I feared my blood would burst its fragile walls, Your presence would be made manifest, and that oh so precious, that worth waiting for an eternity better part of him would upbraid and calm my spirits. Showers of golden honey would inundate me to restore sweetness and tenderness, and I would dream incense dreams so real that the fragrance of frankincense and myrrh would seem to cling to my fingers when I awoke in the mornings.

How sweet it is to be loved by You. And Cecil knew it Father. For You he crossed perilous seas, for you he went seeking untended flocks in a hostile world. He was a brave man. When I told the others where he was gone and why he went, they were not surprised. I thank You for preparing, unknown to them, that corner of their hearts where they know all things are possible with belief. Cecil had been a man among men, he had raised himself high in the world's esteem, but little did they know, and I must confess I, too, did not guess how distant from the exalted glory of his true vocation this worldly success had left him. Though he was only the second of his race to finish the law school, that brilliance he displayed, that ability to outshine the best white men was only humble preparation, toiling in the field which barely tested his greatness. His soul still slumbered, not even dreaming of its trial, of its strength.

That morning I found him gone I confess I was a woman, Father, the most forlorn, pitiable creature in Your wide dominions, a frightened, grieved woman alone. I cried and prayed, beat my head against the floor in futile rants. I was lost to the wisdom of Your ways. Uncomprehending I wanted the time of my need to be Your time to move, to grant my desires. But all things, the best things must come to pass in Your own good time. I was Job demanding and you chastened me. You who took Your son from us in spite of all the good women kneeling at his torn feet. I shook the filth of a puny, sinning fist in the face of Your benignity and compassion. And after the horror came to me I curled my body like an unborn child on the hard floor, trembling because I expected Your wrath, because I had lost sight for a second of the cherished presence of You which had sustained all that I could call life in my body for so many years. I had cried and cursed because Cecil didn't come back. Because I knew that door would never open unless I went to it and turned the knob. I was a little girl on that floor, Father, till Your infinite, divine mercy lifted me and restored what I did not deserve. Cecil's halo, that better part of him made a brand in my soul.

The building of Your Kingdom on earth is like the gentle lapping of the sea against the shore. Souls of men are those almost invisible motes of silt carried to the land with each fluid caress of the waters. Many are delivered by the sea and rest for a moment till that unresistible force which brought them jerks them away. But some, Father, blessed with Your grace, are deposited and stay. To anybody looking all them grains look alike that the water brings in. But some are chosen and lo and behold in Your good time a golden beach stretches brighter than the sun. So Cecil dropped unnoticed. Had his moment with the others. But now all eyes through my humble efforts and the magnificence of Your design shall see him in the true blazing light of his sainthood.

It is no easy road, and it is no accident that some are picked. They used to play ball, all the boys in the neighborhood on Sundays would go to a clearing in the woods, behind where the old sawmill used to be and play baseball with their shirts off. Girls being girls would follow the boys down there behind that shell of sawmill and sit like they was interested in who was going to win. Some of the bigger boys was heroes and always hit the ball clean to the high weeds and could have gone around the bases seven times with their sweaty chests poked out like roosters cock-a-doodling but in those games everybody won. Cause when they were finished some went to swim in the crick and wasn't one swimming suit among that whole mixed bunch that went so you can imagine what kind of swimming those sweaty boys and shameless hussies did. The others weren't no better. Taking their business private into where the strong boys hit the long balls or finding corners in that ruined sawmill or its wrecked out buildings. And it was the Sabbath to top all. I know it is hard to see such a Sodom as educationary for a saint, but there I was one Sunday the first time I snuck to see for myself what I could never get to learn much about from the other girls before one would giggle and blush then all of them giggling and blood high in their cheeks so many hens cackling before they got much past saying *well we watch 'em play* before one would start up.

Wickedness was rampant when I arrived. No innocent ball game ever because there on what they called home base where one stood with his big stick a flaming box that looked familiar burned. Excuse the expression but it was a box of sanitary napkins right out in broad daylight flaming for all that mixed crowd to see and nobody enjoyed it more than those giggling girls, backs just out of church clothes that must still be warm in a closet or across a chair where most of them sloppy hussies probably throw theirs. I was shocked, but like a new fish I had no better sense than to leap for the naked line. There I was almost comfortable in a few minutes, laughing with the rest and waiting my turn on the nasty cigar the boys had made.

Then He came and got me. Your militant Angel Michael with his wings high on his back overshadowing us all. My good Daddy in black and starched white with his hackles risen high as I ever seen them round his tight collar. He was that avenging angel snatched me round my bare arm from the midst of sin. He roared like some mighty bear or lion. Before his wrath even the most shameless scattered, goats and sheep alike tramping on one another to get out his way.

125

And his hard hand on my bare arm gripped tight and hot like Your word grasps my heart. I cried out not in agony I know now, but in understanding, the hurtful recognition of Your strait and narrow path.

He switched me. I felt the air and sunlight rush real fast up between my naked legs, and knew ankle to bloomer, they were exposed to the world. Though it seemed his hand still deep in the flesh of my arm, it was underneath the new red skirt and my two best slips clearing a path for his serpent switch to chastise my loins. I tried to run, but stopped when I heard everything ripping away. If skirt and slips came away I knew his hand would be free to rip away that last cotton between my shame and the world. It was like everything hushed. His roaring, the trees, the sky, the ground I wanted to open and hide me from the others. Just that switch whistling and me sighing too scared yet to cry or scream each time it bit the backs of my bare legs. Not even tears to comfort me. I just stood there in the red, hot pit of sin, stood till I felt myself sagging in the middle and had to go down like an animal on my hands and knees in that field. And when the devil came wretching up from my insides, Daddy pulled the skirt and slips down over my hips, helped me to my feet and let me lean on his hard body till we was home again.

Thorn and blossom, Father, both teach the meaning of the rose. And if the instrument of Your knowledge must blister the flesh, surely it is better received here in earthly fires and in a time that has beginning and end.

Whenever Cecil raised his hand to me it was as Your instrument. I had caused him to sin, to make profane vows. Even in the hours of his darkness Cecil could perceive the load of sin he gathered unto himself, that weight which grown tenfold he would one day have to remove with raw and bleeding hands. As You forgave me my weakness I forgave him the lash, the blows, those hateful, bitter words. On

126

my knees while I earned the pittance which kept life together for us. I prayed each night that he would be delivered from those harsh, secret burdens my love could not remove. I wanted so much for him to move with joyous strength, upright, untrammeled vigor as a true pilgrim fulfilled his tasks and journeys. But the cleansing of his soul rested in Your miraculous hands. I was Martha, going the way of deeds. I always thought of my reward in terms of Cecil's success, in the maturing of my love whether it was returned or not. I asked for no promises. I lived with him as helpmate, as wife, never asking more than the knowledge in my soul that I was achieving Your appointed task, though my duty took me along darksome, unfrequented paths. I knew what some called me. It was difficult and trying at times. There were those who were affronted when I sat beside them in church. I was called harlot, fool. I did not explain to them. You chose a blind man, a whore, even the dead to illuminate your mysteries. My worldly life was public and misunderstood; my life in You was for myself. And Cecil.

But he was a scoffer. I almost smile when I think upon the breadth of Your mystery. How sweet it is. I feared for Cecil's soul, even felt my belief threatened by his blasphemy. I forgot the unfathomable limits of Your mercy, Your redemption that can pluck a sinner from the very jaws of Hell's mouth. Never, never too late. There is no time where You move. Even with his hand an inch from the doorknob, Cecil did not know it was You who called from the other side.

Promises to keep, the fruit You planted in my womb was an earthly promise. Cecil said he wanted that son, that our union needed no blessing but that child. And when I carried him, Cecil ministered to me the way he must have tended Your faraway flock before You in Your wisdom called him to Your side. He was gentle, knowing, cared only for those parts of himself which could somehow enter into my needs. I had only to ask and he gave. I knew the love of one of Your saints. Not for myself, but for the life I carried I asked Cecil for a name. Like the promise in my womb, the promise of a name was given. Two names in fact given to the child yet unborn who Cecil knew would be a boy. Simon Braithwaite. But then You took him. Born and died too soon, prematurely without stock for this world. A pure soul spiraling back to its Creator before even earthly love could soil it. We mourned. The day of our intended marriage passed. Cecil did not speak, barely moved from my bed. Then still with no sign of life beyond the immediate motions of arms, legs, and hands that moved him from place to place, he went back to the law school and his dormitory room, promising he would return and marry me when he had finished.

He did. I remember how strange it was to be with him again. It had been nearly two months since I had seen him. I did his work in the building as best I could, as I do it now to keep this poor roof over Fanny's head and mine. With my arm locked in his as we walked down the aisle, he felt no closer, no more real than from my seat in the back of the auditorium; something not Cecil he had seemed marching in the long, black gown toward the platform where a tall man passed a ribboned scroll into his hand. A long day and I was wet beneath my dress. I wore the same white all day. No fancy bridal gown, but a saint's white cotton I had sewed myself simple and cleanly over the silk slip I saved so long. He remained a stranger when we got back to where we stayed. I had cleaned everything. New sheets, a new picture on the wall, one of the old Italian ones I knew he liked. It was Jesus at the foot of the cross. I knew he would like it because once in a church where we went to hear music he had pointed it out. Said he tried to draw it once himself. But he didn't even see the picture I don't think, and I was so tired I just couldn't sit up with him no longer, just sitting saying nothing in the black suit. He made me think of the dead child and his staring not seeing anything just made me more tired than I already was so I pulled my robe over the new slip and lay down on the cold, new sheets and went to sleep.

He must have turned off the light before he left because I remember just before falling into sleep a red wall like a sheet of flame close up against my eyes. It's like that when you have to shut your eyes against light while you're going to sleep. But it was dark when I woke up alone. Blind shut, door shut, light out.

I dreamed he touched me. I dreamed unmaiden dreams of wind in my hair and against my thighs. I was in water and Cecil from nowhere like a hawk plummets through the air, I saw a dark cliff where he leaped from and he was a bullet about to slam into where I was floating and I knew the spray would dazzle, would burst and make ripples and circles and flowers in the water.

He snatched me, Father, from the brink of perdition. I knew then he was Yours. That Your love would not deny what should be mine. I find I falter, Father. I find the words are not proper. I am a dark spot of ignorance in Your luminous world. I forgive him, Father, forgive him, I am wholly Yours. I ask only to be brought to rest as he is resting against Your bosom. Sometimes I hear his voice. Sometimes it says I am coming, wait. Sometimes it calls me to find him, come to him. I am at times desolate. I find myself again prostrate on the hard floor. But doubt does not throw me down, doubt does not send me to my hands and knees. I want to go down even farther, I want to crawl through the dark earth for you, Father. Forgive. Batter my heart. He died for You, in Your service. For You, for me he did it.

They are singing tonight. When the song is over I will testify to Your goodness and grace. I will tell them how

Cecil served, how he served to the limit of his strength, gave what only saints can give. Do not renounce him. Let them hear my fervor, my words. He is in Your hands, Your hands.

ESTHER BRAITHWAITE

April 19, 1967

What you gonna do when death comes creepin' in your room. The song was a funeral chant, same words repeatedly dragged over a slow, heavily accented rhythm. Words moaned, slurred, stretched so that the beats of the melody thumped with the relentless, painful irregularity of a cripple weaving his way home along a dark alley. Esther found a seat in the rear of the gospel tent. Against the mournful cadences an electric guitar twanged some message of its own. Ridicule, resignation, either the urgent thrusts of a soul being born in spite of everything or the futile challenges of a spirit already on its knees.

THE JOURNAL

March 2 "And did you see the island which is inhabited by men whose heads grow beneath their shoulders. A friend of mine once described it to me." Is he afterall as mad as I want him to be. My Uncle Otis and myself. How many times have I tried to ascertain once and for all the definite point at which his madness begins and the fence rises which is the bulwark of my sanity. He of all people to be the first to whom I spoke. I returned from another country and hoped to find something familiar in him. Was I looking for myself, a mirror.

March 3 It appears that I will be able to remain. It has been almost a year. Not even church brings Esther here. Nothing will take me back to her world, to the Banbury Arms.

March 5 The time is six in the evening. The sky is salmon pink. Birds browse above the threadbare sleeve of river. I can see the melting silhouette of a barge being pushed by a tug. Can they find the sea from here, can they walk on water till the other side of the earth. I am the pied peeker issuing a proclamation. It is safe here for no one listens, there will be no temptation to follow. The sky is salmon. A glob of silver and blood flecked flesh squirms to be liberated. Once, twice, a thousand dashes of its sharp snout against the unexpected rock that glistens blackly in the stream. And it flops weakly till stunned, only its tail quivers, butterfly wings weighed finally by a gush of current, then moving only because the water moves. I am afraid to walk on the water. Of the pale, floating condoms that may still carry life.

Esther was with me when I climbed the stairs to the top of the monument. Oh say can you see. She giggled and spun round full breasts that buffeted my chest light yet full so full I had to press all of her into my arms. Consuming, losing that sight of myself, of the city, of her strong shoulders and the billowing dress she shouldn't have been wearing. We looked down together, side by side, and I asked her if she needed my eyes too, so much to see she smiled and closed both hers saying no you take mine and tell me what we see.

Dinner on the town. Night and getting chilly but we still roamed at home in the city's heart, its steep sided glare scooped out of the darkness. Put your hand in mine. Whistle. We bought a bottle of wine against some future thirst, walking till her feet hurt and my thighs heavy. Bridges. I think we crossed several, over water, buildings, streams of headlights chasing each other. Trees and a place to walk soft under foot; bridge now arching like a roof above spreading the quiet of its shadow so no one could see us. Beer cans tinseled by moonlight, patches of trash that were snow tufts littering the ground.

Esther shivered in my arms. I stopped fumbling with buttons, the flimsy things beneath her spreading dress. No point in letting the night run up under her clothes, nor my hand part of night of the cold disturbing her reservoirs of peace and warmth. The bridge curved above. Traffic a sound distant but within like the roar of a shell clamped to the ears. She said it's warmer when we keep moving so we walked from the shadow toward the river, but though nothing seemed to stir, a chill breathed by the water floated out to meet us, wrapped around her thin calves and took her through the dress as if the flowered material was only another layer of bare skin. Arm around her firm shoulders I took a few steps away from where we had been, inching, edging along the metallic band of water that was not dimpled but sculpted by the diamond-cutting edge of moonlight. Toward the far dark trees, the heavy growth tangling into the water's edge where river turned and was lost. A few steps barely audible her breathing suddenly bird rapid and fragile as her body pressed more closely to mine. I tried to remember to forget, to talk above the night. It was Dowson that finally came in sputters and fragments my mind unable to focus clearly and my lips trembling so the words were painful to speak. Shivers passed between us indistinguishably mine or hers but I could not laugh as we both laughed when in bed naked belly to belly some ambiguous gut rumble oozed from our stillness. Night long in love and sleep she lay. Cynara. Surely, surely I have been faithful.

March 6 The darkness of the ceiling and the darkness of the floor rush to meet each other on the bright face of a wall. One shadow climbs, the other drops, and the colors of the wall disappear. Innocence is a sense of expectation, a belief that certain events will occur, events which are inseparable from personal needs and aspirations.

> I have spent my time
> In pursuit of a fast happiness
> Chasing springs I have never seen
> All those springs happening before me
> Because I was young.

It doesn't matter what we accumulate, eventually it takes on a sentimental value. Is it because we know we must die alone, amid things? Newspaper reminisces over a seeker, an innocent:

"I remember a gentle dreamy young man who started out on the theory (common to schizophrenics) that he had a divine mission to save the world—it's never clear what from. But first a female soul had to come down from God and unite with his soul. There was no sign of this happening, so he liberated one himself, very neatly, with a carving knife."

For the innocent, desire and attainment have not become separate ideas; he feels there is no need to qualify his wish. Until a man has gotten up from the bed of his love-making, pulled off a contraceptive, washed his penis and flushed the whole wet glob of his seed down a toilet, many ideas about copulation can exist that this afterlude banishes forever. The morning after, the moment when flesh parts and there is remorse, sometimes panic. It's different then to wish for love again. Some people forget quicker than others. Some never forget. Rilke good on the instant of separation. How it is difficult to believe anything has happened.

March 8 The Cobra Room. I have been here before. Too familiar too soon. The music, the faithful languid round the magic circle. Lights go on in mirrors, twist around the glass rims. My name is wanderer, seeker. Agamemnon of the whittled host. To my lips soliloquy rises then falls, whispers then lisps in silent, faultless frustration. I am a discard of my mother. Something she grew inside herself and lost in a grunt. Heave ho. The hatch is down, the wave is on the rock, the music is a lullaby. The bar man watches either pleased or annoyed I cannot tell what if anything plays across thick lips, through the eyes that are cat yellow and opaque. Of course I will have another. The season is upon us. April in Paris.

March 9 Sometimes I am very sorry for what I have done. There are times, less numerous, when I am not certain what I have done and why I should be sorry. Leaving Esther and the rest, betraying the people whom I have loved. Or what love meant to them.

March 10 Uncle Otis had told the story this way: Ilyan (some say he was a Jew) was governor of Ceuta, faithful vassal to the mighty Lord Roderic. Ilyan's charge was the keeping of the gate; he guarded the very navel of Roderic's dominions. Poised where he was between east and west Ilyan received tribute on his island bastion from both the sleek, dark horsemen of Africa and the sumptuous envoys from Roderic, though remaining unswervingly loyal to his master. In fact Ilyan's allegiance was a legend men swore by.

Fly in the pie. Ilyan had a beautiful daughter, soft-thighed, innocent pride of her father's eye. Ilyan hoped humbly, but with a sense of the gratitude owed him, that his master would take into his court as handmaiden to the queen the daughter so loved and doted upon yet willingly sacrificed if for her ultimate benefit a lasting union could be achieved with one of the noblemen who formed the king's glittering circle. With overwhelming cordiality but pleading with regret the cumbersome official maneuvering that necessarily surrounded such an undertaking Roderic acknowledged his vassal's request and the matter seemed destined to rest forever in the stagnant swamp of court bureaucracy till Ilyan, infatuated with his scheme and almost desperate with fear that the ripe beauty of his virgin daughter would fade unnoticed and unadorned, journeyed with the maiden to the court on a contrived mission there to let all eyes see his only child's nobility, grace and irresistible beauty. Her appearance in court did what the decades of service and imploring letters to his master had not accomplished. Soul warmed by an inner glowing light and his daughter left under the protection of the king, the faithful governor returned to his rocky island.

In less than a year the arduous journey was repeated. Into his arms the old man took what remained of the fair girl-woman, weeping as she told her sorrow, her dishonor, of the bloom gone never to return. The king welcomed his servant, ravished him with delights of the court, called his loyalty solid as the rock in his trust and publicly put his arm around his vassal's stooped shoulders. Swallowing the black bitterness Ilyan smiled at the peacocks and birds of paradise fluttering around him. He copiously thanked his host, repledged his vassal's oath and as if blind to her red eyes and swelling body took his daughter and bowing returned to the east. But not before, in the height of merrymaking, promising an exotic gift as a small token of his gratitude for the king's welcome. Knowing Roderic's and hence the court's passion for the hunt, Ilyan promised to the revelers *hawks such as they'd never seen.*

There were meetings. His gates were opened and from the east those swift, hawklike men sped into the soft underbelly of Roderic's land. Their thrust was headlong, irresistible, and up and down the ravaged countryside widows and virgins wailed echoing the sound of his daughter's shame, a sound Ilyan had not been able to drive from his ears. Tarik leader of the dark horsemen who gave his name to the betrayed rock between east and west could not understand why Ilyan wept when messengers returned with joyous tidings of victory. Afterall the old governor had offered the gates.

March 12 My hands have not changed their color. I still desire the concealed warmth of other bodies. How can I tell it then, measure face against face, compare the dark shapes: shadow to form. When I left I had no destination. Now I can say that to myself, return and retain that fact in my conscious mind. One suffers to learn. If it is the will of gods which makes things fall out and not the single stubbornness of each living man, then was it necessary to leave? Aren't all voyages redundant, superfluous. On the rented bench of the Paris park, cowering from the pigeons of Trafalgar Square what did I know which I had never known. The world is a small room inside me. No one enters, no one leaves.

March 12 I return to the museum where I met Webb, to the picture. I hear the water running, kiss of air driving the thin jets out of the circular pool. Splash of water returning to the pool's opaque center and rippling outward over the bright pebbled bottom to a border of black marble circling the fountain. Ceiling is high, octagon within octagon rising, trapping footsteps that resound against the marble floor. Eight walls, four doors, four black benches curving around the pool. One wall crowded almost by "Christ Carrying the Cross" which dwarfs two dimly colored paintings of Bosch that flank it. Neither is convincing, not the "Mocking of Christ" with its insect demons and flat gold background nor the "Adoration of the Magi" whose blubber-lipped black king is caught in a burlesque pout. Only one face haunts, Magus standing in carmine gown, the face of the prodigal returning, the vagabond peddler who has tarried and lost his shoe. Faint hint of a beard, of exhaustion around the eyes. Too many days on the road, in the wind, gazing after the chimerical star.

Water climbs and falls, ragged pinnacle of straining drops, then noisy as it troubles the marble basin. I do not think Webb touched me. Only his voice, solicitous, gentle, the promise to perform miracles greater than those hung on the eight walls. There should have been seven walls. I would build a room around a fountain, a lion spitting seven streams high in the air, the beast high on a pedestal whose form would be the smooth backs and graceful buttocks of seven buxom maidens. My king would roar his water magic in seven directions toward seven walls and on each wall the portrait of a sin. Not clustered small on a table top but spread floor to ceiling I would have mad Hieronymus do me Lust, Avarice, Gluttony, and the rest twisting round my fountain.

If you are very quiet and listen only to the water a stillness comes over this marble room. It is a monument, a sepulcher for those bones forgetful of the illusion of flesh. Hard, black benches force admittance, kiss the ischia as in some persistent buggering embrace. The room is full of guilt. Of the sound of urinals constantly, futilely flushed against corruption. He said suffer to learn, he said suffer to lean, walk across the water.

So on that day when it should have still been Esther my new wife on my arm and the sunlight on broad stairs and boulevards and columns I stepped instead acolyte to Webb's phantom lore across the void.

Rogier van der Weyden—"Christ on the Cross"; "The Virgin and St. John."

Gerald David—"Pietà."

Two St. Jeromes and a partridge in a pear tree.

March 14 Franz Fanon: *Wretched of the Earth*. He characterizes dreams of oppressed natives. Dreams are always of

137

muscular prowess, of action, aggression. Counterpoint to behavior native must exhibit for colonial masters. In life, when awake he must be a tree, but night liberates. "I dream I am jumping, swimming, running, climbing. I dream I burst out laughing, that I span a river in one stride, or that I am followed by a flood of motor-cars which never catch up with me."

March 14 It happened a long time ago or at least it is far enough away that I feel it no longer. I think I was a young man in Spain. El Moro. The heat was white and stretched in wavering piles like snow. I could set the scene further . . . detail the music, wine . . . how the castle's geometric walls were sheer . . . the tableau of workmen, their berets, and rope belts, sound of bread chunks breaking, shrill birds fishing in pools of dark moss that floated the dilapidated walls . . . the way far below among the red roofs donkeys jingled past going nowhere. But I am uneasy, impatient at certain times of the year, the fall to be particular, beginning in September I cannot raise my spirits, see or celebrate. As if the fabric that holds moments together slowly begins to tear and disintegrate. Time becomes separate, disjointed fragments leading neither forward nor backward, isolated instants that wheel sickeningly in drunken, futile circles. A hawk wounded, dying. A voice calls *it is time, it is time, it is time,* but I am only the dream of myself and the voice strangles in its own reality.

Only a coincidence, but time is *emit* spelled backward.

March 19 There was a park near the law school in which I liked to walk. In the park were trees, grass, diles of sog phit, bare feet, pregnant ladies, benches, checkerboards, old men, a commemorative rock from the battlefield of Gettysburg, a basketball court, sliding boards, cracked cement walks, trees, benches, women who expose themselves when they sit, dogs being walked, the sound of surrounding traf-

138

fic, black children running down, across, and up a steep-sided gulley in the park's center. At times Cecil was also there, especially when September was more than half finished and the cruelest month close enough to touch, to smell the deadening fumes in the air, to hear the dry hand worrying the trees.

Park of all my springtimes, park various as existence itself, the only way to go for Cecil in his premature, suffering moments. (Sometimes late at night, after the booze and talk among imminent lawyers, there would be a wooziness of exhaustion and floating languor that suddenly for a moment became still, quiet, and in that moment an inkling would come of what a better life could be, might be. The body is left behind. Something rises and surveys. Wisdom, affirmation, peace—all the blood running home in a brilliant tangle toward the sea. Corridors of time echo the black sound of a footfall. You are removed—full of dimension yet dimensionless. You are not measured, but the measure. No distinctions remain. You are accepted, full, filling. But that too was a parklet, an oasis those *sometimes* till human voices . . .) He named the trees after generals, didn't count the blades of grass but addressed them collectively as the multitude. His generals were impartially chosen from all nations, all times. Included because they had done other jobs in addition to generaling, were emperors, presidents, writers, a philosopher, even a homosexual proving that, taken as a group, generals are pretty much like the rest of us Cecil expressed to the multitude one day, but they only nodded.

Consolation was when shuffling through the early dying leaves a rustle could be sustained that held his thoughts high enough so he could see them, a gilded spider web strung against the sky. Remember how the corners of the windows near the steeple's top were molten for an instant. As if once more the glass had been born in fiery heat or was phoenix going home again. Then he had looked in an open window: dark, high-backed benches, stone walls, faint musk of old, damp tapestries hung too long away from the sun. Pipes of an organ. Walking faster while the glimpse entered him. He could have been caught peeking, asked to come in, embarrassed or embarrassing. So he tried to find the brazen images again. But light in the corners was gone, the metallic gray of dusk glazed them sightless. The fire had dropped lower, suffused to brilliant, unexpected patches at rooftop level and along fences, in the chrome of automobiles, or in blond halos insectlike hovering above dark forms. Thought was whistling old tunes, forgotten, truncated tunes, which were never completed because never more than half-learned. He could not whistle, nor recite the words of any entire song. It was melody decayed, enhanced, added to, subtracted from, multiplied or divided by other fragmentary gusts of music. He thinks in the darkness of thought, the complicity of his remembering and not remembering. He imagined speaking to Hannibal and Hannibal answered. Or he spoke to Hannibal and imagined the tree's response.

This park or rather parklet which Cecil enjoyed had no fountain. Statues (a verdurous Dickens being stared at imploringly by Little Nell), but no fountain. Paris parks are built around fountains and Cecil's one reservation about the park near the law school was because of water's absence and the absence of Universality which the presence of water guarantees.

Sometimes he wished the gulley would be inundated. He would warn all the black children, then help them off with their clothes so they would be ready to splash into the water after they had careened down the steep slope. But water still could be a problem. Insects, disease, the repulsive colors of stagnancy. The vision had really not been of a tiny

140

lake, but of the sea. Of pot-bellied, large-headed, grinning pickaninnies galloping across hot sands and being taken by the salt sea. The grass is greener? What is sea green, sky blue? What are colored people? Wine dark sea?

The park was amusing when he was lonely. Either it or walks by himself (along the river front, through the city's eighteenth-century streets) or hunched in some theater seat hoping the camera slips that the censors slipped, that in one sublime frame the hair pubis will appear dark and tangled like the lowering forests beyond which barbarians live their rampaging lives. Time was when woman real, woman flesh private, obtainable over time at slight discount filled my nights. Not those fantasies orchestrated by snores, grunts, and wheezing silence of old men, starved men, with hands in their pockets or hands strayed to past time, time to come, prostitutes, substitutes, the stale familiarity of their own private parts when the getting was good. Getting better all the time I can walk among the trees, along quiet streets in strange neighborhoods. I can avoid the warm, yellow lure of other lives framed in unshaded windows. Walk, mind my own business. I must read Robbe-Grillet. His book about a voyeur. French movies, blue flicks, girlies, stags. When you've seen it all somehow the titillation ceases, there is something funny about the holething.

The young lawmen called her Briar Patch because of the abundance of curly pelt protecting her lower middle. A bush it was (and burning one of them revealed, blue ointment in hand). All of them agreed it was unique and after much consultation Cecil was summoned and permitted to judge and agree. In the darkened room he peeked beneath the shade across the fifteen feet or so that separated the law dormitory from the nurses' blindless windows. She was best seen from Carpenter's bedroom, and when the show began, he called the others to take their turns. Not only Briar

Patch but her roommates performed. Cecil laughed because the others did. Cecil went down on hands and knees because the others did.

March 20 Dante's Bellacqua, condemned in Purgatory to sit beside a rock and dream over his life forever. His punishment for sloth while he was living. Cecil as Bellacqua at the window? beneath the trees? beside the fountain? Now.

March 20 Nightmare. Early morning. Dampness, soft sucking earth. A thick tailed, heavy muzzled, gray dog. Tree like flame. Yellow leaves in the center, gradual deepening of color till leaves at periphery of tree's outline are flame red. Unnatural rapidity with which leaves fall. A multicolored, swirling snow. Movement of leaves gives form to the wind. Like hair blowing can be urgent, disdainful, flustered. Tangible motion, something that is swift, invisible being born. A shark's inevitable meandering that dramatizes the medium's presence.

March 24 It is spring, earth rendering spring again.

Morning April 19

So spring comes again.

> "Silent as a mirror is believed
> Realities plunge in silence by"

My journal is strangely blank at this season. I believe I was once accustomed to write poetry. Spring made a lyre of me.

When I get up it is birdsong and walls gleaming that should be but are not quite opaque to the sun. I know it shines, that the day brilliantly begins. I have plans, desires. Quickly as God is my witness I shall begin to undo what has been a winter of slothful discontent of faltering and hesitation. Urgent this need to be fated, to be hooked by the taut string.

If that is me staring back. I heard my feet pad, across the wooden floor. They must be large, fleshy. I always wear a T-shirt when I sleep, only when another's nakedness looms beside me do I strip away the last covering and even then I know where it is while we rub and romp and sweat and when we are still and either one or the other has cleaved and turned away I reach deftly for it to cover my sleep. An old pain, fear of night chills and stiffness. A physical fear of what it might be like to waken stark and unprotected, the ache too late to dread already inching through deep back muscles. To shiver and know it is too late. The fear is that which comes at the end of dreaming after the crime is irrevocable and I am a captive.

I cannot remember having the dream last night. Peace plundered. Perhaps changing as the seasons changed. No longer March dream of violence, rage. Have you held a life in your hands, twisted it, darkened it till something not life slumped from your fingers. Oceans of blood whipped by the moon and winds rush headlong to crash against the skull's echoing walls. The body lies there divided from me. It has been prepared: laved clean, suffused with the ripe glow of its own fullness. She is not beside me, not behind or in front of me nor lying motionless neck awry at my feet. Someone has combed her hair, demurely crossed her ankles and laid her hands softly along soft hips. More than ever the image beyond reckoning. I would crawl to her over seas of broken glass. More living than ever (how wind stirs the web of short, curly hairs) I know she is more alive than ever but I am caught and condemned, have been chased breathless and cannot speak while they say guilty of death till death do you part till death.

My big bare feet. Someday I want to meditate on my

143

body. I will study it, then logically divide the several king-doms. Write an elaborate description of each member. Toes, thighs, knees, fingers. Measure everything precisely, designate color, texture, even count the hairs, chart their relative frequency. I would leave a plan, a map. No, they will say, this one is not an undiscovered country. He did not lose himself in a futile chase after the seemings and changings of the mind. His record is a real one, his exploration valid. He knew himself and now we do too. Someday they may reconstruct me. Homo sapiens c. 1950 (extinct). This model based on writings of Braithwaite, Cecil O. pioneer in science of Self-Knowledge. When a coin dropped in the slot I become animated, immortal. I am programmed to act out their image of their swarming hotblooded ancestors. I am speaking a quaint English and my exaggerated, frantic movements are those of a nineteenth century Shakespearean actor.

From the mirror. If I am the pure form of myself, the super reality of me then how am I to treat you and the million forms you take. And do you diminish me. And when you are in her eyes is she killing me. In a crowd am I losing something invaluable, irreplaceable even in the stares that do not see. Gathered round me like a flock of ghosts. Imminent children of the imminent father. I am what.

You see

In the mirror

Returning do I create a mind looking back. You have a white T-shirt just like mine. Do you sleep in it always.

Hair grows after death. As do fingernails. Even after death to be shaved, manicured, pedicured as if something still depended on the living as if it does now. I have been tempted to grow a prophet's beard, to forsake soap and water. I am a cliché unto myself. Saying, doing the same things, the blood things I can disguise but not change. What was never thought and only poorly expressed. Sum of being.

Another said when it's poetry you cut yourself if thinking of it and shaving. O O O you Shagspearean rug cuddled round my chin. The storm, the hot gates, cold steel, warm steel, steel too hot *señor* you are about to burn.

> Roses are red
> Whiskers are blue
> Poetry's your face
> Looking at you.

Not bad for an im-prompt-too. I could rhyme forever, never ever lever sever fever. Eye rime. But this is bathtub shower shaving poetry. The kind calculated not to bite. Am I rite. You see when we are talking of things serious and wish to communicate I believe there should be rules to facilitate the message. I propose more silence, a quiet stretch after each speech as Cooper reported his Indians to observe at their council fires. I would propose that no one speak until he can rime his first line with the last line of the preceding speaker. i.e.:

> 1st speaker: And so I conclude.
>
> (*Pause*)
>
> 2nd speaker: Perhaps you wish to delude . . . is all
> I have to say.
>
> (*Pause*)
>
> 3rd speaker: I agree, but would put it this way . . .
> etc.

Etcetera. So it would go. The improvements in verbal discourse would be immediate and profound. First each speaker would have to listen closely to his predecessor in order to earn the right of reply. Secondly the pause would make him organize and ponder his reply. Third the spirit of poetry, wit, and repartee would preside over even the most traditionally pedantic and unimaginative occasions for speech. A new class of rhetoricians would grow up. Imagine the impact of a speaker in the Senate who could end a perfectly appropriate and reasonable argument for abolishing war with the word zebra. From such a context would arise the golden age of Philosopher-Poet Kings. Great men who could only be followed by silence or consent.

Steam rises. I see only shadows, lemur eyes lost in deep sockets. The flesh melting. But if I lose you, if you die, another, another will come. Steel is the temperature of my blood. It is congruous, her soft hand that caressing glides down my cheek, a finger traces the bottom curve of my chin, my throat.

You are so easy. I do not cringe, shy away. I have been waiting for you and now I kiss your finger that is crimson tipped.

Spring is all things blossoming. Sudden bosoms and bare legs, that corpse we planted last fall. All the young men who have learned to cower and die who have not learned to ask why they are dying, whose chests will be heavy with medals, ribbons, and flowers tropically lush and quick in the loam of gristle and blood. Spring before summer and summer sin heavy because we cannot forget. The chorus of Argive elders, ghosts of winter, snow clump preserved in the high shadow of a mountain we had not intended to climb. What is their foreboding what unseasonal talk of prophets long dead of omens fore-telling and fulfilled long ago. Certainly they did not expect all this to be gained without loss. Without sacrifice. They murmur as if they never knew someone must pay for spring. Each spring. All the time I suppose they thought it was the early dying ones, babies, young men. They grieved, they were assiduous in their lamentations, they made a song of mourning and dressed in dark, choral robes. As if they didn't know that would not be enough, as if all things did not have to suffer. As if they believed the suffering and sacrifice were over. But here it is spring again, all things relentlessly blooming and

146

the elders wonder why they are not touched, not made whole, why roses do not blossom at their lapels. Why age does not drop away.

My face is smooth. Mexican hairless. My fingers draw blood wakes. Five knives slicing forehead to chin. How long do you want to live. Can you repeat yourself. If I carved ever so carefully, surgically flayed away one layer, what would I be. And if I lopped off an arm or a leg. My head?

You are the sum of parts. Some Cecil replaceable, others mysterious, inviolable if you are to remain whole Cecil. Chemistry of addition and subtraction. What became of Cecil in her eyes. The steam. *Give me your heart my love* must be looked on with even more suspicion than before. Discreet, vulnerable parts. The shame of obsolescence, the purring intimidation of better machines. I am a nest the young have flown. I am dry, the dull bits of me are carried off by the wind.

If the walls let in light then perhaps within me is not as I had imagined. Styx dark. Black capped waves restless lolling above the black sea invisible against the black sky. Years, millions of years of distance to be traversed, the black sun weeping on the black land. Perhaps instead the flesh is an infinitely subtle prism, perhaps the blood laps multicolored, multifaceted, jewels within a kaleidoscope. Perhaps I could live there, float on my back in warm amniotic waters quietly fascinated by the circus of lights.

It is the flesh, the body I fear for most. To be handled, to be molded like putty into a mask of repose, to have cosmetics applied to restore color, to be falsified, violated, shaved and washed and manicured even after I have lost the power to be ashamed, to decry, despise, cry, or laugh over the ritual. To have other hands do mechanically what I have done with agony and determination, because I saw the doer, what he must do. That meeting of eyes when mine do not secure

147

his image. Coins on my eyelids. To be as powerless as a child who has his favorite toy taken away, the mirror taken away, the ghosts locked in the machine.

No poetry but anyway the blood blooming sudden buds on my upper lip. I am closer, magnified. I am watching the jet's shadow stumbling beneath me on brown plains. The shadow grows gradually less distinct, a blur, then nothing. Red ball of sun sucked in a matter of moments below the broad, flat plains. Patchwork, colorless quilt, monotony broken only by the irregular gashes of dark rivers and straight, shaved highway bands dissecting the dun and gray on which low clouds cast their illusory forests of shadow. (A square of toilet paper drinks the blood.) The land is mute, humble, acquiescent to the elaborate swirl of a partial cloverleaf, to the symmetry of baroque, concrete curves. My man's scarified skin magnified ten million times. Approaching Chicago. I have seen the epidermis pictured thusly. A patchwork desert of unimaginable, rutty distances. Ringworm of psoriasis twisting dramatically through the submissive tissue.

Blue in the distance. Am I hovering dead over the land. What is dying on the ground.

Carefully I clean my instrument. Beneath the glint of stainless a fringe of hair is obdurate, will not be dislodged by bursts of steaming water. I will not use my fingers in the dangerous slot. Already I am looking for blood spots on my grainy upper lip. I can see the Virgin where she always is, stony on a pedestal that leans her precariously toward the earth. She is white, or better, a dingy gray standing in someone's backyard. I have chased children from her. Their rocks had snubbed her nose so a buddha's profile stares vacantly at someone's back porch. I think she is lifesize. A boy had to reach up, to plant the fatigue hat over her cowl. A graceless, stubby virgin yet artistically placed among the high, rotting fences, spilled garbage and heathen weeds. I have seen the moon on her forehead. A white smile.

Hail Mary. I must remember to watch her when rain is falling. A gray day when the slants of rain are thick and distinct, when the water seems sent to cleanse. I could take a picture of the drowning Virgin, of her gray indifference. That would be before she ascended to the kingdom. In fact the precise instant before her trip when human all too human the deluge began and she without brolly or rubbers. Absence of rubbers (prophylactical contraceptacle as found in most dirty men's rooms) has been the bane to Virgins time out of mind. *Stabat mater dolorosa.*

Your hands along my cheeks. Take my face, mother, as if a prayer had suddenly dropped from heaven and wedged its thick way between your steepled hands.

Dogs, cats, and children go in and out of your shrine. The sky is a roof to your temple. I have seen you all hours of day and night but never have I seen you asleep nor ever preparations to disrobe, bathe, and lay you down in the cool weeds. It is your stony duty I suppose to remain as you are, weather the weather, flinch not from dog pee, cat pee, boy pee, or even those small hands that fondle your stony breasts for a second before they seek to topple you. The boy who brought the hat also moved his hands in and out of your stone robes. Adoration. Would you take a black lover.

Sweet Life. Sweet Simon son. Laid to rest one day of spring, invested in her silence in her flesh soil embedded was my son. I can dream of rivers of freshness, of sunshine holiday. Blue coming in at my window tells me all that season has not been forgotten. Charged blue like something glowing in a child's paintbox which he goes to first and spreads indiscriminately over the printed designs in his coloring book. Pretty, pretty blue.

But you would not recognize the color, the day. No seasons for my son. I am sad but perhaps at some level deeply relieved. There has been and will always be color. The last rot of the last man will be vaulted some season of its passing by blue. And warmth and snow in passing. Things that fall will kiss and cover, brush by and race the heap to oblivion. All this glory to the insensate, the putrifying last trace. So your eyes, your nose, your lips have missed no rarity. My son I couched you within her, November, and wish I could say the day, the hour, because I was desperate. You were not to be simply the glue between Esther and me; we needed no bond or perhaps knew no bond could hold us together if not that identity of will and blood we had become. No, you were to be something better. A contradiction I suppose to the way the earth seemed to be turning, to what I knew myself to be and all starving men to be. I wanted you to be full, complete, not a living hunger or a word written in the sea. I was oppressed. Three hundred years I had been stooping and dying, the life urge dribbling out obscene and curdled like white insides from a squashed bug. I could go no farther. Backward nor forward, neither side to side, just stand and dance in my chains, teeth showing not in joy but agony as my ankles were rubbed to slender, trembling roots ready to snap and end the jiggling dance forever. I studied the law.

All so simple. Someone always there to whisper *Cecil you are not real*. That is no body swaying but sunlight glancing from steel braces caught in the shimmering heat. Do not weep or moan. You are not there. You are not real. Smoke.

Cecil, let me tell you how it is. This girl, young pretty and white, she come up to me smellin' good, wearin' nice clothes, trying to smile. I want to help is what she said. Then all the sudden she got puffy pigeon breasted grew ten feet and sprouted these stiff gold tipped wings. So I begins to move a little closer but them wings start rustling, hum-

150

ming and glowing around her. She gets brighter and whiter and them blue eyes crackling so I freezes and stops thinking what I was thinking. Wonder where the white girl went.

And can you imagine asking someone to dance and actually dancing in a crowded ballroom when you are a black face and there are no other black faces in the world.

Well, to be short, simple, and to the point, Simon, greed, fear, hate, and ignorance, the outriders of the End, stocked the land. The best people were already being suffocated by the high, thin air of impending doom, the premature apocalyptic putrefaction in the bodies of the people. The best men hadn't slept for years. Echoing through their consciousness night and day the death keen of King Agamemnon lacerated ear chambers where rest and comfort should reside or the sea sound of echoing forever.

In my desperation you died. All thought of providing more fuel for the fires of hatred and destruction was impossible. When we loved it was always with walls, the rubber sunk in her womb or the drooping dunce cap crowning my root. And though in my fury and need I coupled often with her, still when alone I would grasp it in my fist and shake and choke as if this one time this final brutal separation would be the last. I waited for a drop of blood, an excruciating pain or sense of relief, some sign that all potential for life, all possibility of providing one more black victim had been wrenched from me. I cleaved life from our thrashing and flesh need. Only violence gave our love-making depth, an added dimension. A thousand, thousand times you died and in my frenzy I was a cannibal feasting on the flesh you could not become.

But early one November, again I regret the lack of detail, in my desperation death brought you forth. Impossible conjunction, nature's mistake as much as ours, you were conceived.

Simon, can you ever forgive.

Of course it was spring. A day not unlike this maybe. Across the land there was mourning. Men and women in black march among the tender, blushing colors of life tentatively renewed. Spring is never certain. Always the possibility that its delicacy, its ethereal forms will not make it, will be false, cruel omens not of summer and life but of that unrequited yearning in men's souls that leaves them shivering on street corners in thin clothes at the mercy of sudden arctic winds. Maybe, just maybe, is the moan beneath the rush to enjoy, maybe it won't come, this will be all that we will get. Hurry, hurry.

But the mourners were stately, solemn in their pavane beneath mimosas, tulip trees, pink and white early blooming ones. The king was dead, long live the king. At this impossible moment, at this almost melodramatic gyre of epochs cycling to a still point and prophesying in their dying pinpoint glimmer the configuration of the future, at this death/life, black/white, peace/violence, love/hate extravagant, metaphorical, metaphysical moment of truth you could not wait, you chose to rupture the membrane, the sheerest curtain retaining wall of all, Simon, you began.

Was the timing perfect; sublime in its irony and false promise. With the portents running so high and prospects darker than the thought of black men when it first occurred to Mister Whoever is Responsible for All This Shit, what would one expect if not a life for you that touched the outermost edges of tragedy and farce. A life that would be the fullest sounding board of human experience. And so I rejoiced. In spite of myself, after the most profound sleep and death, life was being resurrected. Life as a thumb in the nose at impossibility, life as a redemptive, unquenchable force outside of me, outside of things. But Simon my son you came too soon, never even got a breath of fresh air.

I am willing to go on. I will breathe, shave, fuck. I will be a man of all seasons. But I will not undam those squiggles of other Cecils, other xy Simons in my loins. No, the black man was not meant to be. Ask them, any of them. *You are not real.* And unless some God comes down and starts to kissing this black clay again it will crumble and blow away ungrieved, unfollowed, and without remorse.

Bitter, am I bitter on a spring morning Sweet Life alive just outside my door. That cannot be. Surely I have learned to forgive. Afterall Cecil Otis Braithwaithe. First of his race to do, to be, etc. You proved something, Cecil. You are in fact the only one of your race. There is only one black man in the world. Love him. He has no brothers, no look alikes, not even dogs to be loved in the bargain. Just say *I repent.* Just say *I forswear all rights and privileges.* Just say *They are not real.* Real is Cecil, real were those fine white men your classmates and what they do and what you will do as practitioner of the law. Nothing good comes without sacrifice. Christ paid for our sins. Let *them* pay for their own. Don't you know *they'll* only drag you down, eat you up, Cecil. Being one of *them* is as impossible, frankly, as is being one of us. That's fact, it's written. I kid you not. Just look at the realities of the situation. Whose sins do you care to die for?

Choice one: *Them*—dying for their sins is dying for nothing since they are unreal. Proof of this unreality is a choice you can make, a choice which can make them unreal. Forsake nothing.

Choice two: You—you are one of a kind. You will be treated accordingly.

Choice three: No choice: an illusion founded on a misapprehension of your other choices.

Now to go through this picking and choosing routine every morning is time consuming. In fact it makes you very inefficient, in fact it is a leaning toward choice three which is of course an absurd choice even in some ways more absurd than choice one since at least a blind, dumb passion for martyrdom bogus or not could be argued as a reason though not justification for choosing *Them*. Why teeter-totter like a mindless child? The assurance of company on the other end of the seesaw board? Could be a rock, a weight set there to fool you as well as wear you out. Come man. Choice two, choice two is unavoidable. Everyone likes to be thought of as unique, don't they. One of a kind, treated accordingly.

They are testing the sirens. In my book there will be a siren. Shoooooeeeee. How does one represent a siren sound. I need it. What better background for the Armageddon scene. And its fitful foreshadowing wails that will be a leitmotiv through the novel. Wheeeeeeeeeeeeee. The scene in which my hero is walking through the park contemplating suicide and he whistles a dirgelike keening monody that is picked up by the mournful wheezing of a factory horn then the whine of a jet till finally a throbbing banshee cacophony swirls around him in ever widening circles and his breath dragged by the tail of his whistle is sucked from his body and he is nearly hysterical till freed by the rumbling of a trolley car that wraps him in its trembling nearness.

For a movie sound track not a novel. In my journal when I want to catch some mood, make some point, I wish for the MGM orchestra. A crescendo here, violins soft in the background, there and there a trumpet salute. And pictures. I cut them out and paste them in the journal. But my novel.

There is no novel. I have a vivid imagination, and countless frustrations. Therefore I retreat to illusion, fantasy. Call my imagining my novel. Journal as close as I get. But not even journal, more like . . . like nothing but fantasy, illusion. My notes to Simon, my prayers unaddressed and unbelieved even as I pray. I write my novel with my backside as it puts down roots in dusty movie house chairs. My book is all the things I spend so much energy preparing to say to someone but never do to anyone. I am seeking the one word book.

154

The *mot juste* which ends all imagining, all squirming, all encounters with the eyes of old men in cages beneath lurid marquees. Cecil.

> Birds fly good days or bad
> Birds fly because they are sad
> Bird or his heart thumps at my window.

Window. Skindough, shindough. Chin though. Pause. Something maybe. Pause. Scrunch forehead. Dig deeper worry lines.

Bird won't shave my chin though.

Cecil's face is clean. He leans toward the window. Virgin still there, smiling in the sun. He can hear the children coming.

Afternoon April 19

Terrain spreads rusty, grease splotched redolent of barbeque, fried chicken, dried blood, waiting to be blasted, cooked, done by these allegorical hands my brother. Currycomb through layer after layer then somewhere cringing beneath (last layer of scales, sores, turf to shock a phrenologist) is the roots' base, skull wall thin but hardy Walt would you feel it if I bite steel teeth into your cranium. Yeah, yeah I know it hurts but that's the treatment, brother.

At the door is Gin Brown with Pepsi-Cola and chow mein.

–Hey Clyde baby, you got to do this thing.

I should have been a camera. Pretty pictures and no memories. Snap. Snap.

. . . and this is Walter Willis' head, before and after. Quite a difference, eh. Like between being seen in a Cadillac or in a Ford. How many pimps you know drive Fords.

. . . and this is Walter Willis, first potato of the day dropping in the bubbling fat. Let me advise you of something Walt. These hands about to be violently laid on your head are the hands of a man who has scaled Mendelian ladders time out of mind from tiniest spoor of salty rot past sloths and killer apes past Pithecanthropus and your Neanderthal experiment. Walter I have highwayed my way straight and narrow to this last whining spiraling exhausted dead end. I thrived, I fed on green pastures, pastures new reserved for the experiment I was. In the beginning was my end. Like those anthropoids that dropped from the trees too soon and could not learn the reptilian lore. Swallowed as the earth bathed in fire and ice. No canines, Walt. They had to chew and grind all day to survive. Daisy eaters, pansy eaters, eaters of the rose, daffodils, lilacs. They drink no blood, Walt, had no wine no Tiger Rose Thunderbird Pio Manischewit₹ Gallo Virginia Dare grapes and so they salvaged nothing from their dispossession only when they were dying did the high flying days return, vestigial, blurred, nostalgia as being devoured, a predator relieving the hot secrets of its bowels, glazed monkey eyes of the victim on his back last thing being seen was thick trees swaying, swaying through a mist.

Like this forest I have raised atop your head. Crested in front, a crown of tarred feathers for the king.

—Brown, this shit is cold and the other shit is hot.

Mr. Gin Brown unnerved because unbaptized because dry trembled in all regions of his body, those seen and unseen, he stood on the porch of the Big House waiting for Marse Jim, never a hungry water bug caught black and ugly in the middle of the kitchen floor was more petrified by sudden revealing glare of light than Gin Brown needing this drink bad and thought he had made a hustle but cold hot food and warm cold pop flopping if only I had that one that

straightening one pull me together get me together get it together that one that one.

—G'wanne Gin Brown. You ain't nothin', nigger.

Brown bent to catch the dull thud of dime on the check-
ered linoleum. No, he don't look disgraceful down there
trying to get his shaky yellow thumbnail under the coin's
edge. You blame a piglet belly-sloshing his way through
mud to get to the titty.

Wine dime now or wait and get enough together for gin.
Brown tottered at the threshold; the dime burns through
his clenched fist. Dime wafer offered to his lips.

Blood, Walter.

—Whisky kills you, wine make you crazy. Pays your
money, takes your choice.

—Gin do both.

—I know when Gin Brown make one hundred and thirty-
five dollars a week. Long bread.

—He got too good for his old lady. Put her down. Always
in Oscar's. Fast cat.

—Fast. That nigger was Speed hisself. Dance his ass off,
too.

—Good old lady. Would'a made something of Brown.

—Put her down. She always called him Clarence. Oscar'd
tease her. *Is Clarence here? Don't know no Clarence* Oscar
would answer grinning in his dark place, but all she could
see was his eye through the peephole. *Is Clarence here?
Don't know no Clarence.* And then finally she would have
to say *Gin Brown Gin Brown is he in there, please, is he in
there.*

—Dance his ass off.

—And Oscar would turn laughing. *Is there a Mr. Gin
Clarence Brown in this establishment.* And everybody
would laugh and know she was on the other side of the
door and Oscar would say *Nobody by that name here.*

157

–Made something out of him.

–I seen him count it one hundred and thirty-five clean. Thirteen tens and five ones that's how he'd always get it. Bet dollars one at a time to learn his luck then nothing but fading tens till his gone or everybody else's gone.

–Fast Gin Brown.

–Speedo Brown.

–Dancing Brown.

–Ten dollar Brown.

–Pay the boss poor hoss lost.

–Ten you don't ten Brown.

Ten can't wait, wine dime gotta do it cause used to it got to get together.

You are Walter Willis and for seven dollars and fifty cents the difference between being seen in a Cadillac and being seen in a Ford.

–Clyde baby, like how you mean, No.

The laying on of hands. Cecil Braithwaite touches the hair of Walter Willis. Gingerly at first then down to the red roots chafing, greasing, handfuls of slick wool stiffened by an occasional wire bristle. Knead, finger tips on skull. You can feel the tar wedge its way beneath the fingernails. You remember popping string beans, the perforated belly bowl and when finished handfuls lifted and then cascading lean and lumpy sound of rain back into tin bowl. The white oleo in bags. Lard white but a red bubble on the side of bag and you burst blister red seeps, spreads beneath your fingers like a bland dawn sky into which color oozes, blood bubble squeezed till everything is soft yellow. I am buttering your dome. Pure vegetable coloring no one will know the difference. Which twin is bologna. A lady never tells. Only your hairdresser will know.

There goes Dr. Sylvester. Dr. Alonzo P. Sylvester in his Continental.

Constance Beauty's was filling up. On the floor dark ir-

158

regular matting of martyred locks. On the ceiling gleaming white tiles. On the walls mirrors, mirrors ricocheted the room from plane to plane, doubling, tripling, devouring. The shop had seven chairs and often all seven would be occupied wafting their tenants in lifts spins twists and bends, positioning them so each customer could be subtly accosted by comb, heat, and chemical. On this spring morning April 19, 1967 at 11 A.M. five chairs danced, four black sheep being shorn, the fifth transfigured to a wolf.

Hot already. Sticky enough outside and the shop predictably ten degrees worse. Five attended customers, five attendants in white, three customers waiting and eight spectators kibitzing in various attitudes. Constance Beauty's was one large rectangular room, its glass doors opening in a short side. A curtain separated the back room from the arena, and as needed potions, balms, and unguents were fetched from the other side of the drape by the white coated acolytes. Only Process Pete's was competition, and long ago the two shops had partitioned the territory, not by a geographical division with its inherent difficulties of border watching and dissident minorities within the artificial boundaries, but by a simpler economic expedient—Process Pete's charged $5.50 and had to itself beginners, one shot artists, the indigent and transient needing a blast, in short those who really couldn't afford the luxury, but were hooked or in the process of being hooked, those who had fallen from good times and those who would never reach them, while Constance Beauty's $7.50 price catered to those who liked to give the impression they shared none of the crimping necessities of Pete's clientele.

Cecil spun his chair catching for a moment the sublime repose of Walter Willis' sweating face. The rivers of perspiration were appearance only, deceptive in their hurry and confusion; what Cecil saw beneath the film of change and impermanence was soul, pure soul. Walter, head afire, scourged of the flesh, Walter spirit supine at the foot of the swaying lotus trees. Oh how happy you have made me.

Dreaming Cecil soaked and singed absorbed in momentary flights of fancy which he communicated to the tarry jungle of Walter's head. Under Cecil's deft fingers Kilimanjaro rose, the horns of a bull, cuckold's horns, the Eiffel Tower, the twin peaks of Marilyn Monroe, anonymous buttocks and phallic symbols. Consummately these artifacts were created atop Walter's brain and just as resolutely when they had reached a formal perfection, a leveling cruise of the comb extinguished them forever. Dead without a trace, a phantom world above Walter's skull, a *tabla rasa* afterall was said and done. Cecil thought of ripple making, that other transitory art he had conceived. Since the artist can only call the process of creation itself uniquely, truly his own in a manner that not even the finished, public manifestation of that process is his own, the most pure art and the one perhaps most satisfying would be the most ephemeral art, the art that was all process, all unfolding, all experience, the art which removed the necessity of an exportable, finished product. Not a new idea certainly, but novel and revealing to Cecil as he sat beside the still Italian lake and tossed pebbles into its sunclean surface. Each pebble, depending on complex relationships among force of contact, angle of incidence, size, weight, shape of pebble, and countless other factors mysterious enough to form an art, produced a distinctive ripple pattern upon, within, and beneath the quiet water. Sun golden bands crept outward from the initial brilliant ring. The possibilities were endless and the challenges a limitation not of the medium but of the imagination of the challenger: size of rings, speed of rings expansion outward, perfection of rings' shape (a badly thrown pebble splashed so that the circle's shape was pitted, distorted), more than one pebble would be thrown at a time to achieve subtle rhythms, interlocking patterns of ring with ring, shadow with shadow. And a moment after the pebble had struck, after the creator's eye had been delighted or depressed the entire effort silently passes to oblivion.

Fulfillment rarely and if it comes at all, unified too closely with the process to be exhumed, made a monument. The creator whose canvas will always be naked, unresolved, ready. The black, bright lake kissing Cecil's mood but gone before the embrace.

Before the laying on of hands.

Suppose I made of your fleece a wedding cake. Seven tiers, Walter, and on top lovers arm in arm. You would have to let your hair grow even higher before I could attempt such a masterpiece. Let it be ten feet long, each strand a bamboo pole stiff and erect. The world would wonder why. Why so tall Walter. Why so tall. There would be talk, betting pools but finally the day you entered Constance Beauty's, talk and smiles would cease altogether. They would gather in droves outside and invitations to the privileged would allot the inner space. Cecil of ripple fame would at last divulge an example of his heretofore transitory art for the delectation of the public. Until Walter's hair went back home or was rained upon or he forgot his stocking cap and mashed the sculpture while sleeping, the multitude could experience in their midst a frozen artifact of the most essential art.

Seven spiraling tiers each like the Grecian urn decorated with a frieze of classical scenes. Seven ages of man the theme, culminating in naked Adam and Eve resplendent on the crown, their proud private parts promising a new beginning, a continuation of the cycle. Walter, the ebony Atlas, would balance it on his head. And each day the world floating elegant, graceful and precarious down the Strip. Niggers knowing to fall back, not to touch, to look but don't leap as the world is carried past.

161

Cecil ripple maker, coiffeur supreme. Creator of an art that has no past or future, no tradition to be sustained or transmitted infinitesimally modified to generations unborn. No corpse poised along the chain of straining, uplifted hands.

Ripples begin and ripples end. Ripples are made then gone. Cecil is a ripple playing through the increasingly recalcitrant hair of Walter Willis. A wind ripple that in slow motion disturbs and stirs the fleece. Swirls, mounds, caves, a landscape exists then doesn't exist. A past is either present or not at all. Walter sleeps.

–Here comes the Continental again. Drop top with four doors.

–Nigger has all the money in the world. Least all the money down here the number man ain't got.

–You talk about pills doing a job. That nigger done scraped away just about as many babies as he brought into this world. Charges $300. Wish I had a dollar for every fixing up he's done.

–You think you'd get tired of looking up pussy.

–When redeye stopped winkin' back I'd get tired.

–All pussy's the same.

–You's a lie and a grunt. You sure ain't been round many if you say a fool thing like that.

–Black, white, brown, yellow, I been all over the world when I was in the war and up holes every place I been and I'm telling you pussy is pussy.

–Smells different according to race. And white ones ain't so hairy.

–You got it ass-backward fool. Them German girls and French ones got hair niggers ain't even thought about.

–That's European women not white.

–You are one dumb nigger. Never been out of the Strip, a chitterlins and cornbread coon.

–You sure think you know something. I been places. All over this goddamn city. I know something you don't. Where

162

I'm wanted and where not. Who my people is and who ain't. I don't kiss no man's ass just to get his white smile on me. And the stuff he's tired of put in my hands like I's supposed to thank you boss thank you boss and shine his shoes. And European ain't white.

—And you are not the descendent of an African, I suppose.

—Oh no, here we go again. Africa this and Africa that. And black, black, black. Nigger, you're makin' me tired of being black. Robes and bushy heads.

—Why don't you be white then. Go on, be like Willis. Watch when he gets up out that chair with his good black man's hair all straightened and waved. He won't be black any more, Willis paying $7.50 and he's Tony Curtis.

—Seems like it would fall apart. A car without no top and four doors.

Cecil combed and curried, smoothed and patted. The reddish brown roots of Walter's hair were invisible, hidden beneath a coat of glistening, contoured jet. Roots were where a bad job showed. Like shining the toe of a shoe and leaving the sides cracked and dirty. Getting at the roots was probably the most painful segment of the treatment for the customer, and a minimal singeing of the cranium would be rewarded by the well-heeled *cognoscente* with a generous tip. Cecil's caution in dealing with Walter was perfunctory. No sadism, but no financial considerations either to crystallize Cecil's concentration. He burnt and wandered, swimming in what was now a din of voices within and cacophony of activity outside the glass walls as the Strip sprang into full, loud life.

From the Avenue Record Mart the Staple Singers entertained the mothers who were shopping. Later it would be the Temptations, James Brown, Stevie Wonder and those stars of lesser magnitude who would hover above the Avenue, a radiant canopy for the teen-agers returning from the mountain where the piper leads them six hours a day five

163

days a week forty weeks of the year. But in between spirituals and dancing music, the dispossessed were serenaded with their own special kind of music. Late risers, nonrisers, the men who would make the action after dark or men who had been flung by the action onto these barren afternoon beaches would listen to a potpourri of cool jazz, West Coast jazz, blues, oldies but goodies, dead musicians, throaty dead singers, the static on bad recordings lacing their voices like the night club smoke and unerasable tinkle of glasses, low warm talk, Lady Day's last live recording.

Sleeping, somnolent rhythms. The sudden screech and crash of a subway, a match flaring in an alley, a bottle crashing to the pavement. Knife sounds, hurt sounds, sounds that were taxis' wheels gliding to rendezvous. Cages locked, cages flung open. Litters drawn by matched leopards, stretcher-bearers in white. Constance Beauty's.

Constance Beauty's had a jukebox. But on principle it never competed with the Avenue Record Mart. No more than the Establishment envied Process Pete's its medium to full house, its register ringing $5.50. Afterall some presiding, ulterior force guaranteed the smooth running of the Strip, perpetuated the profound rhythm of its identity. Chord and Dischord. Advance and Retreat. Violence and Peace. All factions, contradictions, extremes not extinguished but harmonized, not blurred but made compatible by a force whose nature Cecil could not plumb. Was it blackness, some secret experience of the race, blood knowledge ineradicable. And would it always be so or could this knowledge run thin, exhaust itself in one mutation of genes, one black coupled with white or black ridden by deeper black. Was the Strip a ripple, blackness itself and all its secrets a larger ripple in the infinitely slow, infinitely bored game playing of time wasting time.

Cecil's fingers slowed. He walked away from the chair, eyes straight ahead on the drapery, the only surface that did not return his image. Though he focused narrowly on the velvet curtain and though his ears strained to be stones on which the breakers of sound would crash and subside, Cecil could not turn back the sensuous reality lashing about him. Smell taste touch sight sound all his and not his. He was their excuse for being and they were his excuse for being, for calling this memory Cecil and that one Cecil, and all those things Cecil upon which he had no claim. They claimed him.

A Swiss lake, or was it Italian. It didn't matter because what did matter was how aloof in the quiet, in the stillness in the abyss illumined only by pebbles' bright plunge. The moment said . . .

Do I shuffle, do I try to hide as through the gantlet passing of mirrors and eyes I am afraid of seeing myself in them but want to be there want to know I am someplace seen that I am substance, that the sea parts in my passage, that between knife prow cutting and fan wake Cecil can be seen Cecil is neither one nor the other neither becoming nor gone as a foamy wake is gone. Must I see myself in them to know myself to believe myself. And when I awake from dreams must I always fear the larger dream, circle within circle, Chinese boxes forever insidiously, diabolically enclosed, ripples within ripples.

The deep voice from the jukebox made him start. But then quickly other voices, the bitter-sweet Miracles, Bill Smokey Robinson *et al.*, the lilting, swinging rhythms yet always that trailing edge of poignancy of loss and regret barely concealed that was the Miracles' style. *Tracks of my Tears.* Afternoon music. Who played it. Cecil saw no sign. But the Miracles singing, the tile, the mirrors, matted hair on the floor.

Because the singer smiles . . .
They smile
What I am is what I feel now. What else, how else. But Webb took me and pointing said this, all this is yours.

Museums, whores, all the beauty he thought was me, all

165

the beauty he thought. And I was young. I could kill the
dragon, release the golden dream, find the cup, the maiden,
the castle, the home, the father, the seeking. Ruins, ruins
we all fall down.

See a clown's face

An entertainer

And though I have made mistakes, he confessed, though
I have betrayed, even slaughtered believers, in fact had least
tolerance for the best men, though I have been wrong, there
is beauty in struggle in a past no matter how gory, how defiled because it is a past a child to the man and though your
body is among those gored and defiled . . .

But the blue song inside

And though she suffered at my hands and though he for-
sook me and disappeared . . .

His eyes remembering

You are not my son not my flesh but heir to my dreams
to that better part of me laced with greed envy bitterness
and fear though it is still a better part . . .

Ghost tears

Old sorrows walking down his face

Walter Willis yawns and stretches, receives Cecil's final
ministrations and with serenade rather than coin of the
realm tips the magician. Poets pay that way, why not Walter. Briefly Walter beside the chair and new Walter in the
mirror coincide, couple, exchange places.

–Kiss my ass, Clyde.

Night April 19

Go back. Go back. No matter where Cecil found himself
sooner or later the admonition to return would slink then

dance to his ear. Go back. Return. Reprise. Repeat. About face. Again. Return. The direction was clear, but destination, even point of departure impossible to grasp. Ring the changes. Sea changed. Sea-borne wrapped in hazel mist, swaddled in pea coat, balaclava, rubber boots the boy stood on the shining deck. For he is a Charlie good fellow. He is afterall a victim of circumstance, of circumvention, of circling, curling woolly locks. And keyless Cecil weeps at the command. He retrieves from its hook the tiny brass bell. Ring a ling. Ring a ling. Life buoy. I am held up by the waves, they fondle my arching prow, they foam wash me. Why are the niggers moaning. Why do they fear this voyage home. Ring a ding ling. Lifeboats in order. The deck is clean, the hold hosed down. They should shit less when they don't get much to eat, provisions are low. Do not cry my brethren. Tell Martha not to moan. We are going back, we are going home.

Uncle Otis, please tell me a story. Listen to a story. Beneath the cautious street lamp that slipped an arc of salmon pink around his shadow, Uncle Otis stood resplendent as if in a suit of lights. Wary Cecil approached.

–I am confused, that will be apparent. I want to start at the beginning. . . .

–Why me.

–It's necessary.

–Who besides you could benefit from the telling.

–You are an amanuensis, a recorder.

–A pawn then. Benefiting not at all. A plaything. A device. Taking advantage of your old uncle.

–A necessity. A necessity because so far there has been no story, no telling, and I must begin. You see, when I walked out of the door that evening, I had no idea. I was just . . .

–Taking a step.

–A step then another and another. Somehow it led to

167

him and the need to tell and I suppose the need to return, to begin. My mind plays with me. Retains, withholds according to a will that is seemingly beyond me, outside of my control. I feel exploited, manipulated by a force I cannot fathom. And yet I am the meaning of the force, if its reality can be known I *am* the force. But he . . .

Dark night. Listener chews his gum. Itches near his groin but will not reach down. Sees Cecil in a tree.

—You are waiting for a monologue.

Nod (anything, nothing, beginning, end, motherfucker. Just do it).

—The night I left I didn't touch my wife. No good-bye anything. Kiss, caress, word. Just Cecil gone into the night. If I could tell you about that night. How it felt, how much I lived in the first few breaths of black air maybe the rest wouldn't be necessary. Remember what I'm trying to get to. Why I had to go through the door. Perhaps I was just sorry for myself. The bad luck. Perhaps that long flagellation, that impossible lifting of Cecil by Cecil, the learning of the law, that see, hear, smell, taste, touch, say, be no evil monkey I had become chased me through the door. None of these, perhaps. Just blackness seeking blackness, beaten by blackness. All those Cecils *I couldn't be* calling the ghost I had become. Promises. Promises. The ones I made and ones made to me forgotten if I got through the door. Well as it turns out those first few breaths of black air at the beginning had in them all I would ever learn. Now it becomes a word game. Shuffling them in and stretching and straining and exploding till I can say it tried and I tried but it was not quite it, not the word because something essential still missing still asks to be propitiated by another word.

So night is this which is unavoidable, inevitable either as it bursts through the narrative or dies one of its seeming deaths just out of reach but always always there. You see I could call myself night or call this night my foreknowledge and thorough knowing of myself but that would be to make a rounded, full tale I have never lived through, nor anyone lives through, until knowing that rounding will not come the need to erect it comes into being and then a scaffold rises as much air and space as it is orange, cool tubing and we say out of courtesy there it is, the emperor is so well dressed today.

As I recall I kept on my wedding suit. I must have put the jacket over my arm as I walked because the day had been so warm that night made no difference same heat but different because it seemed stale, walked in, sweated in like someone else's sheets you find yourself trying to sleep on but they already have given all they have to give, exhausted those frail possibilities of habitation and they either smother you or expose you refuse your measure within the ghost mold of the one who has already been there. I walked and tried to find some cool empty place but of course I did not have within me any sense of seeking or search just the inertia of one foot after the other it must have been hours or days I walked out reserves I had not known I possessed, I tapped resources of purposelessness I had resigned myself long before to being born without I stitched oblivion with unknown, untiring steps as if there were a state of undreaming between realities and I could plunge deeper and deeper once I stumbled into it.

I have no memories, no images to share. Have you watched the caged animals leave their cells in some distant gazing that is through you through walls an irresistible, hurtling stare until you can see fur dissolve and teeth crumble and the high stench incense burning for one departed, lost even to itself far away in jungle, cave, or black river you are dizzy and fear disintegration because some part of you is in that stare, swept with it beyond cage and sensory evidence that all is here and well and organized as it should be to the end of that longing that roar of the eyes dissolving

169

lion flesh or ape flesh your flesh and ridden home where the blood waits to be consumed. As if I could become the sound of my feet, and in the same way physical energy can be drained, I walked until what I was, what I had been began to collapse and run away in salty streams beneath my black suit.

–The meaning of this is that I need you to listen. Authenticate.

–Piece together.

–Not that. Not help. There are no pieces. I could accept fragments, shards. No. Just listen. Listening assures me that something has transpired. That I began and ended. Something in between.

–But that night was nothing, was steps. You see why you must simply listen. Add nothing, make no effort to construct, construe. I told you night was everything, that it was me, that it was the story. Now I call it nothing.

And it was nothing. Can a man listen to himself going to dust. Surely an instrument delicate enough could record the *gigue* of ashes to ashes. A thunderclap when heart beats one last time, how that note would linger, the accumulated resonance of ten billion remembered beats, linger like clarion knell over wing fluttering palpitations of near silence as nothingness gestates within the meat and bones slowly gnawing, gnawing at substance, molecule by stilled molecule meat to matter to bad breath in a wooden box. Fetus of nothingness full blown in one gasp swallows all memory all trace of ever beating ever alive something gone nothing. There should be applause when the music finishes, wing systole and diastole, but no man can listen to his own dust and no other man could clap in such final silence. So I didn't even listen to those footfalls I know I was, but I know I was walking toward nothing and perhaps beside me umbilical I drew him or he drew me two in one trace one echo we *moved together* because those words can mean from immense distances from no knowledge of one another though nearly touching back to back two nodes on a huge circle we began to approach a confrontation, each drawn steadily, magnetically around the circumference of the invisible circle, or the words mean side by side, juxtaposed, paired, twinned, walking two peas in pod as invisible to them as the circle around which they move together.

No one face or voice or building or street can I recall. Only when I stopped or seemed to stop did I begin to take account, to estimate where, when, why. So you must keep in your mind that this is guesswork. Reconstruction after no facts. A long time somewhere because when I stopped, I smelled, was filthy, bedraggled. I had a beard. My feet felt as if they had been bound in rawhide to stunt their growth. I could not talk easily. A kind of hoarseness, an unfamiliarity with movements of tongue and lips, with the shuttling of spit and breath at the proper intervals. A craving not for food but for water. Nausea faint, slightly threatening at the thought of food, an inability to even conceive of individual foods because some effluvia haunted my throat and I could taste and feel its stirrings in my belly, a gaseous distillation of all food, the essence of food which was the color wheel of all foods spun at a rate that blurred the spectrum to an oppressive gray. Whirling total presence or absence of everything I had ever tasted. But water I thirsted for. Needed like I had once needed a god, cornucopia of abundance to refresh everything from dry lips to soul's desiccation.

When I found a fountain I drank deeply. Teasing, compromising myself with cool, extravagant mouthfuls, swishing the water over my gums and teeth, enjoying the plash against my puffed cheeks before I spit the too much out. I had visions of all the cowboys and legionnaires I had seen rescued from the desert. The rescuer's sympathetic but firm refusal of more than a mouthful. The exemplary caution; too much too soon not good.

171

Then I continued to search for water. This too a paradigm, a compression of the story, like night contained everything so does searching and water. Where did it all end. By the sea by the sea by the beautiful sea. And begin. With the *Mayflower* or even sooner Dutchly planted in this land. *Desire* the ship.

Not only something to drink, but a place to be received, embraced, revitalized. I could cleanse stains from the flesh, whitewash my soul. I was sea-borne as I knelt at the fountain, baptized as I dipped to drink again. Water washed me, rivered me home. I found something was shouting inside me, some excitement unbearably titillating yet promising an impossible, excruciating further titillation. All this in a few mouthfuls. And then simply, dully the first step was over. I was through the door.

And on the other side a consuming thirst. A day blue but overcast and the hour must have been early because I remember being nearly alone as I walked along a beach. Gray sand, warm, full of jagged shell fragments then sleek like an animal's wet coat, gleaming sand pocked with debris. Puddles of foam like soapsuds quivered where they had been deposited by the lapping waters. Frothy and white, some strange animal form, ephemeral, perhaps deadly, miniature glaciers that slid almost imperceptibly back toward the waters that brought them. Wind sculpting the suds the way a man toys with the foam on beer. I was there dreaming of a sea plunge, of drinking and bathing of sun and breeze of salt smarting in eyes and lips but clearing, cleansing old wounds. Though it was early, riders had been there before; deep half-moons carved in the sand, dung heaped so neatly I thought someone must have aided nature to build the golden pyramid near the water's edge. I didn't see them till I had walked two hundred yards or so away from the water. Sand was loose, I floundered, my steps were heavy and awkward as if my body suddenly found itself imposed upon by an unfamiliar gravity. Four riders on shaggy maned, long tailed mounts and a black boy behind them straddling a donkey. The horses bunched together, a frieze of motion against the seascape. They pranced, stylized almost, one body in relief and many tails and manes and legs beside and beneath it to give an illusion of other bodies. White breakers beyond, rippling, prancing, churning to touch breast against breast, to plunge together in one synchronized flurry of arching mane and tail. Splash of hoofs as they crash into the surf, troubling a sea mist around slender ankles. The riders held their reins laxly, giving the mounts full head. And the course of the band and the trailing donkey was erratic, aimless yet rhythmically attuned to the same miscellaneous certainty of the waves rushing to the land.

I stood and watched them until they disappeared. Horsemen on the sand. Riders to the sea. Phantoms who left miraculous indentations and golden piles upon the beach. I asked myself how real they had been, if I had only seen whitecaps dancing across the blue water. I now knew the form revelation must take, and yet I was no nearer, still thirsted, still had some aching reservoir to fill.

Magic water rubbed across my face and the litmus change of young to old man as I watched in a mirror.

Fountain trinkling in the vaultlike room. Pebbles that were pearls. The master crucified on the wall.

So when he asked . . .

So when he asked I didn't even hesitate. Of course I'll go. Night and water there too. I actually thought that thought because the pool into which the fountain dribbled was rimmed in black marble. I had learned to read things, to put them together according to the subtle yearnings, the incalculable forces expressed in what they had lost to become individuals. Or at least some such facility enabled me to be impractical, to forsake my characteristic fear of obvious consequences and embrace the immediate, assuaging effect. But I must not be too analytic, precise about a state that will not bear much precision. I said yes and the rest followed.

–So you went.

–Yes, across an ocean with him. Seemingly in tow, humbly mounted, almost careless about the course, yet like the black boy on the donkey a guide of sorts, and of course like him responsible.

–My prosperous, ambitious nephew, Cecil. Do you remember who gave you that name. In whose namesake, Cecil. Who brought you out of the darkness. I could tell you stories, stories about your name, about darkness, about being dipped in a pot of colored water like an Easter egg. But I know you are impatient. Got a train to catch, don't you. Pay no mind to your Uncle Otis who gave you your middle name. Crazy old coon, gonna die soon.

Cecil Otis pumpkin pie/ Never knew he had to die.

Singsong lament tired on his lips old man leaned against the lamppost. Long, straight spine picked clean of flesh only seven stark vertebrae climbing its sides, the pole drew night closer to the salmon pool.

–There will be a time when you recall all this. How I stunk and my breath so bad you kept backing up as I spoke, and how I tried to move closer to you so as not to have to shout. You'll remember me shouting till I got hoarse and you moving away but never far enough so you missed what I was saying. Like a beating you know you deserve so you don't fight back. Let me tell you something. Like I told it to the whore spitting and wiping her mouth trying to get the pee sting out. If at first you don't suckseed . . . is what I told her after wiping and zipping and ready to go out the door. You should have seen her sputter and spit. She came at me finally, clawing, tearing, screaming to get tooth or nail planted in my black hide, but I was tough and quick,

174

not a mark on me. I batted her butt-naked on the floor and dared her to move. She knew she had crossed me. Turning everybody on behind my back then coming nibbling at me like she was loving and obedient. Mad as she was, I took a chance, though I knew it wasn't a big chance and unzipped again and sprang it in her.

—That name, Cecil, is a slave name. It means hard of seeing. So saying the old man picked from his dusty neck an intruder.

Dies Irae. Tempus fugit. Etcetera.

The hard shell cracked between pressure of thumbnail and first finger.

—Did you see the smoke, nephew. I done the little bastard more good than he was intending on me. Soul mist rising to join the atmosphere then floating till it finds some new form to seep into. Maybe an elephant or a horse he'll be next. Something grander than either one of us two-legged monkeys. Sometimes I think this pole is leaning on me. I feel like if I move away it will come toppling down. When I was younger, I used to love to climb utility poles. You know they have spikes driven in so you could giant step right to the top. From up there things were a lot different. Course you had to be careful. Wires and humming and black boxes I never dared touch. But it was good just sitting secretly up there where nobody could touch you. Sometimes I even thought no one could see me like I had really disappeared from the earth. You mounted those spikes with long stretching steps. Up until the sky closer, the wind louder like sea shells on your ears. I was scared sometimes, but really sorry they didn't make poles no taller.

—I'm going to go back to her, Otis. Nothing has changed. Never will. What they did to me that afternoon. I'll do it. She'll be my wife.

—There are days now when I feel like climbing. I believe I could get up, but the coming down would be too much for these dry bones. I can see the niggers gathered here laughing they asses off at the crazy coon hung up on the utility pole. I had a dream once. I was talking to a dog, nothing silly or unnatural seeming about it, we was just talking. I don't remember how it was whether he was standing or I was on all fours, but anyway we were looking in each other's eyes and having a damned interesting conversation. I remember now how it was. He was on a table, a big stone table and stretched out talking in a dignified voice. The strangest thing was when he finished I stroked him with a big ax. Not vicious or violent or mad at the creature, just did it looking straight in his eyes, and he never blinked or cringed. It seemed the only thing to do when he had finished talking. Butchered him afterward, real professional, like I knew what I was doing. He looked kind of pretty, the way well sliced roast beef looks pretty when I had finished and arranged his skinned parts on the table. Put his still thumping heart in my pocket. It was warm against my thigh as I walked away. When I finally got to the top of the pole (which is why I'm telling you the dream) I was naked and the heart was gone but my leg was moist and stained red on the thigh. When I woke up I had wet the bed.

—Esther is going to be my wife. Not a lawyer's lady, but my wife.

—That's what you said just a minute ago.

—You have nothing to say.

—Don't doe-eye me. After all you're a man aren't you. A man who knows so well where he's going that he's always in a damned hurry. Too much of a hurry to listen to a dying old man.

—You'll be standing by this pole when my children are dead.

—That's what I mean a hurry. You're counting your children already. Geronimo is what them paratroopers say

176

in the movies when they's throwing they asses off into the
wild blue yonder. All Otis has to say is Geronimo.

–Geronimo was an Indian chief. Also a holy man who
lived in the desert with a lion. Who was buggering who I
never could learn, but one went to heaven so it must have
been true love. Then there are niggers call themselves lion-
men, Masai lion men. I won't speak too harshly of that
heathenism. One might be my great granddaddy prancing
around the jungle roaring till his throat is sore. Geronimo is
the last word said by a hell of a lot of men.

–I guess I've got what I came for.

–Did you ever want to be a blind man? Something about
the mouth and mind seems to be improved by being eyeless.
And fingers become better. When he jabbed the brooch in
his eyes he knew what he was doing. The only way he could
understand, could *see* what had happened was darkly.
That's why they are afraid of us. See darky run, run darky
run. They understand what they've done; it's not me but
them that can't forget. Cecil.

–I have some scripture for you. One of the woolly bal-
loon heads gave it to me yesterday. He was talking about
roots and past and the pendulum swinging back. Told me
to come to the Temple, get off the corner and come to the
Temple to hear how wrong I've been done. He thought
there was something being said that I should hear. I
laughed at the bushy top. If I went in their Temple, it would
be as a speaker. I could talk about roots and past about a
black world and black men the woollies had to forget
before they could begin their ranting and raving. Someday
before I die I may tell everything, tell everything then
climb up my pole and watch the walls come tumbling down.
My voice would be a host of trumpets, relentless and shattering. Tarik and his hawks would raze the city, gallop
through here like ten thousand dusky Gary Coopers. A

trumpet and a drum. Drum made from skins of the martyred. Black skins stretched taut again after wrinkling around the starved bones. On the first note they would rub their eyes as if awakening from a long sleep. Their bodies would be tired as if they had been journeying for days. But the sleep haze would go and the exhaustion would flee before the drum and trumpet. Surely good music would follow them all the days of their lives. Globe trotters come on to Sweet Geronimo Brown, scourge of the earth. Hawks such as never seen before.

Otis hesitated, hand on the first rung:

Onya manas. Then like a madman I will shower flowers in all directions. Whatever I see I will worship. Horsemen gone to a pure cloud of golden dust. Sons of Light cascading over the earth like sun after the storm. There are more worlds than one. More to come and many we have forgotten, but they are all One.

He begins to climb:

Lila, is it only this? Does God exist only when my eyes are closed and disappears when my eyes are opened. No, I am not blind and still the rumble of the horseman saturates my heartbeat. The Play belongs to Him to whom Eternity belongs, and Eternity to Him to whom the Play belongs. Some people climb the seven floors of a building and cannot get down; but some climb up and then, at will, visit the lower floors.

Otis is enthroned:

Pitha. I hear the humming, feel the damp throb beside my groin. As from a tall mast silver threads glide off into the night. All things converging, power, peace. My hand is on the black box.

Cecil reads the crudely printed card handed to him by his uncle.

And slay them whenever you catch them, and turn them out from where they have turned you out; for tumult and oppression are worse than slaughter. And fight them on until there is no more tumult or oppression. Koran 2:191;193.

Shower flowers. Cecil cringed inwardly as he watched the trembling old man search for something in the periphery of darkness. Perhaps it would be a large, bruised petal his kneeling uncle would lift toward him.

–I can't find the bugger. Big one he was though. He would have popped loud as the crack of doom. Felt him crawling down my arm and brushed him off before I thought what a treat it would be to float another soul for my anxious nephew. I remember the preacher navel deep in a swampy creek ducking the black bodies while the sanctified chanted on the shore. I would not walk in the water. I hid till the others had to go, then watched from a tree them being dunked like donuts in that coffee-colored water. Maybe it was crystal clear once and gone sour from scouring souls. I think some believed everything would come out white; sin, ass, and giblets if they prayed.

The man stood tall now, no longer shaking. Cold wind in which he shivered passed to the night. Looking at him Cecil restrained the urge to scratch, disgusted by the silent life teaming within the old man's clothing. Like old skin he cannot shed, that is corrupted but will not molt Cecil said to himself staring at the rags loosely hanging on his uncle's body. Suit of lice.

–You are my namesake. You are the only one who came to see me when I had the run-in with the police.

The visitor's window, thick dull glass. The swaying sheet of ticking in front of which the prisoner stands. Proximity of all the windows. Snake house in the zoo. How one must shout to be heard, confusion of all voices attempting to reach behind the glass walls. Babel, din, bedlam. One must bend his ear down to the talking grill. In this position impossible to see prisoner's face, to be seen. Makes commu-

179

nication faceless, mechanical like talking long distance on the phone. Difficulty in hearing, in being heard, seeing, being seen brutalizes the interview. Someone had begun to sing a hymn. Otis crying.

—I could tell you stories. I have a gift. I can handle flame, touch men where they burn and not be burnt myself. I could write their epitaphs. Yours would be Geronimo.

The old man's performance visibly tired him and when he was tired, he seemed to Cecil to smell worse.

—When I rub my eyes it is to see you better, Cecil, to make sure I have returned. How long have you been here. Or rather how long have I been here. There is a distinction you know.

Cecil was annoyed with himself for believing the pole had leaned, had been about to crash down before his uncle's hand returned to steady it. Esther was waiting.

—I once knew a dwarf. Well not exactly a dwarf, but a child who was not really a child but an old man who had grown up too fast, in a matter of months from twelve to fifty then died of old age right there in bed. He said they called it progeria, growing up too fast, all life passes like a film at the wrong speed, days are hours, months, days, a year might stretch to a week. His mind was storm but some days there was calm, he could talk a moment. I lost my job at the hospital because I did nothing but hang around at his bedside waiting for the lucid minutes. His voice would come from far away, a man's voice from the wrinkled old, new bundle of flesh he had become. He said:

—*In me all things occur with unbearable intensity. Never a pause for my emotions to rest, for some experience of my blood's growth to become quiet and calm before the next tumult begins. My whole being races, is scourged by time. Always losing and dying without even the illusion of possession. I cry because I cannot have this illusion, because it is an illusion, a nothing, and yet you are blessed because you*

*have this nothing. I cry for an illusion, for deception, for a
lie to deceive me. I cry because I must tell myself this lie
would be better than my body's truth. I cry because I am
not made to live the lie.*

I didn't dream this dwarf man, neither his clenched baby
fists nor the choked, panting of his voice when he spoke. He
wearied me nephew. I grew tired watching him die so
quickly, just as your hurrying makes me lose my breath.
Go, go to her and the rest. You see me here, where I have
been, what I brought back and what I have. They laugh at
me and they'll laugh at you. They see in us only themselves,
and because they are what they are, can only laugh at themselves. I kissed the dwarf when he slept hoping I would be
infected.

Cecil did not look back once his legs began moving. He
knew it would be a pillar of fire and that he should be
turned into salt.

At midnight when Esther was sound asleep, her Aunt
Fanny quietly slipped from bed, dressed in the darkness and
tiptoed into the kitchen. The old lady had heard everything.
Her niece home from the revival tent, the padding of her
heavy body on bare feet across the boards of the rugless
bedroom floor, the bending squeaking bed, sobbing and
snores. Esther had flushed the toilet twice in the short time
before sleep. I don't know what she could be doing but I
hope she has left everything neat because the others will
soon be here.

When the lights came on sudden, so bright after Fanny's
noiseless gliding through the hall, there was a scurry of
sleek-backed roaches returning to their nests. Not really
many nor overpowering just enough to make some things,

the wooden backed sink, shadows along the oven door that never quite closed, move that weren't supposed to have life of their own. Fanny watched one disappear beneath the blue fluff ball of her slippers (given by Esther at Easter); she looked back behind her callused heel to see the crushed nougat but there was no spot upon the floor. Not enough left in me to squash a bug. No wonder I'm so hungry (Esther screaming eat, eat) terrible pains in my belly, and moving nimbly the implements were gathered by her knitter's quick fingers. A pot and lid for rice, skillet for the fat meat and big boiling pot for the kale. Implements chosen and displaced, Fanny rummaged in the cupboard and icebox for contents. Lined them on drainboard: Uncle Ben's Converted Rice, fat meat on waxed paper, cellophane bag of kale. With a blue-striped cup water was carefully measured into the pot and pan. Skillet sat warming on a low flame. All in readiness the cook squinted at the hissing gas jets to gauge the heat generated by the fine yellow flames.

A moment for coffee which she made by stealing a cup of water from the large pot. Greens wouldn't miss that little bit of moisture she naughtily tapped. Hadn't missed it all these years she had been preparing supper and borrowing her water for instant coffee. Can hardly wait. Turn off the flame a moment while she drinks. These men home later each evening. Thin legs look strange naked for a change since she had left the opaque stockings hanging on chair back in her room. I wish there was something I could sing, that I knew the words of (Esther hates my songs). If she ate now the men would not like it. Not as if they'd make a fuss or anything of the sort just that them out working all day and having no womenfolk about they appreciated that restful hour at the dinner table and her eating as well as feeding them after that long day in the fields. Her men. Her Henry and little Henry and Thomas and Amos and Benjamin. All men and all twice her size. Dark, strong men and her high yeller as anybody in the valley. They liked that too, their woman with bright skin and eyes that were green in the right light. She could tell how proud her husband and big sons so she would sip her coffee, watch the pans, and wait.

Benjie would play with that braid. How pretty your mama's hair Henry said to the boys and they looked funny and didn't know what to do but little Benjie right up on my lap and took it long and silky in his hands. Henry knocked Thomas to the ground when he heard the boy had sassed me. I cried with my Tom, and Henry just standing there shaking.

All day I have so many things to do in this house I'm just so busy keeping it clean and my hands full with all of their things I never think about food must go all day sometimes without passing crumb to lips but then soon as I start to getting their supper ready I get so hungry I feel like these pots full of food won't hardly be enough for me. (Eat Fanny eat, you'll starve to death, fool.) But wait I shall, light the fire, listen to the simmering and boiling and turn the fat meat till its brown and . . .

When Cecil entered he used the same key he had used three years before to lock the door when he left. He heard no sound, saw there was someone in the chair, and for a long moment the insides of the familiar janitor's apartment trembled giddily before his eyes refusing to believe him, to be believed. The body in the chair did not turn. Twig arms and legs told him the form was not Esther's, never in a thousand years would her flesh wither as close to the taut bones. It was Fanny, Fanny grown even less substantial than the doll creature he had remembered. One waxen arm was stretched onto the tabletop and the other was lost somewhere in her lap. Her hair, lusterless and dry, thinning but still with its longest strands reaching far down her back was loosened from its accustomed braid to spread faintly like weeds beaten by wind against her thin back. Nothing moved.

The table was set for six, orderly, meticulous, as formal as the battered china and dull utensils could carry the effect. A tall pitcher of water stood in the center of the table and at the head a frayed Bible beside the fork and paper napkin. Fanny still hadn't stirred and deciding she was asleep Cecil switched out the light then moved quietly past the stove. He left the old woman where she sat, head slightly slumped, one arm stretched to the coffee cup, the other buried in her lap. He remembered swiftly. The element had frightened him, seemed impossible from a distance to manage, like the sea when he thought of swimming alone at night. Terror, shivering, unimaginable phantoms would wait for his foot to break the restless surface. He would be swept away, screaming. But once there, surrounded, submitting the element would care for him, buoy him, reminisce with its hands on his body of peace and a soothing control. Plunge, unhunch the stinging shoulders, glide. He was home again, he would be welcomed.

It was his darkness, his room. He knew where things were, believed nothing had changed, and so it hadn't, and he moved efficiently, not unduly cautious, not afraid of butting into things, upsetting what might be precarious, disastrous. The door he had opened, never to return or to return in a moment or to simply open and see the other side. It moves on its hinges. Is he coming or going, is it opening in or out. The bedroom's one window, cut high in the wall was barely above ground level. To see in from outside you had to move very close to the glass or kneel down. Cecil could see the wooden platforms that supported the outside garbage cans of the ground floor tenants. April moonlight curled around the bottom of the aluminum drums. *Walpurgisnacht*. A black cat with arched, prickly back should suddenly appear, a flood of gray rats thud in terror from the cans. In the

184

harsh theatrical moonlight framed by the narrow window all things seemed possible, begged for some ominous display of the black powers.

Esther's plump buttocks claimed a moondrop. She must have been sleeping when she struggled from beneath the covers because the night was neither hot nor humid. Cecil sat in a straight-backed chair aware of clothing that was draped on the seat and backrest. A moonspot, then moon modeled to the deepened cleft. Wherein joy of my desiring. Stirred. Cecil strained his eyes in the darkness. What would there be to see. Perhaps something I had seen before, perhaps I could see more deeply, she would lead me where to look.

Cecil in the chair, Esther sprawled naked on her naked bed. Moonlight, starlight, the silvered drums trembling imperceptibly as mute, indifferent spirals twist through them eternally. So Cecil dreamed.